North to Freedom

Karen Meyer

Sable Creek PRESS

Other Books by Karen Meyer

CONFLICT AT CHILLICOTHE

BATTLE AT BLUE LICKS

MISSING AT MARIETTA

WHISPERS AT MARIETTA

Cover and text design by Diane King, dkingdesigner.com
Cover photo: © appletat | iStockphoto.com

© Scripture taken from the King James Version. Public domain.

Published by Sable Creek Press, PO Box 12217, Glendale, Arizona 85318
www.sablecreekpress.com

Library of Congress Control Number: 2015936132

ISBN 978-0-9890667-9-2

Printed in the United States of America.

edication

To the brave helpers of fugitives on the Underground Railroad, and the ones who rescue those who are enslaved today.

and

To Jesus Christ, the One who looses the chains of sin from all who believe.

"Jesus saith unto him, I am the way, the truth, and the life: no man cometh unto the Father, but by me."

John 14:6

How to Get Help

Contact the National Human Trafficking Resource Center

1-888-373-7888

The National Human Trafficking Resource Center (NHTRC) is a national, toll-free hotline, available to answer calls from anywhere in the country, 24 hours a day, 7 days a week, every day of the year in more than 200 languages. The NHTRC is operated by Polaris, a non-profit, non-governmental organization working exclusively on the issue of human trafficking. We are not a government entity, law enforcement or an immigration authority. Perhaps you can be a link to help someone to freedom.

Contents

Swing Low, Sweet Chariot

Simon Anderson Farm, Maysville, Kentucky

Spring 1855

The night had been too short for Moses and Tom, and they were still bone-tired. They dressed in the predawn dark and stumbled out the door with the others. After roll call, everyone split into two groups. One group headed to the Big House. The field hands crossed to the iron pot hanging over an open fire. Twelve-year-old Moses spooned himself a bowl of mush.

His cousin Tom squatted beside him. "Grampa saw Master Simon talkin' to the auction man yesterday."

Moses frowned. "Who be gettin' sold south?"

"Any what makes trouble." Tom shoveled in a huge bite.

"Like you?"

"Yep. Cyrus has it in for me. But maybe you, too."

"What day be the auction?"

"Next Friday, at the Maysville Court House."

"What you gonna do?"

Tom glanced around, and then whispered, "Run. Grampa told me to."

"All by yourself?"

"Two's better. You come, too."

Moses shook his head. "No, sir. We get caught, Cyrus whip us near to death."

"He whip you someday anyhow."

The crack of a bullwhip cut short their whispers. "Get to the field, you sniveling laggards," Cyrus snarled. "There's plowin' to do."

Aunt Bess, Tom's mammy, strapped her baby on her back and trudged down the trail. She began to sing, her voice mingling with the trilling of mockingbirds in the bushes. "Swing low, sweet chariot, comin' for to carry me home."

Soon all the field hands joined in singing. Tom belted out the song's question. "I looked over Jordan, and what did I see?"

The rest sang the refrain. "Comin' for to carry me home."

Moses joined in singing, "A band of angels comin' after me, comin' for to carry me home." *I sure want to cross the Ohio. But it be such a wide river. How we get across? Do I run with Tom?*

Fresh earth smell mixed with sweaty mule smell as Moses guided the plow behind Ol' Pete. With each furrow he completed, Moses counted a reason to run off with Tom.

Cyrus be ready to whip me, just 'cause he can.

Maybe Master sell me downriver.

Two be better than one, if we run.

Free folks can learn to read.

After lunch, Moses had trouble getting Ol' Pete back to plowing. Then he sat down to take a stone out of his shoe. Cyrus stomped toward him, calling him ugly names. He slashed the whip across his shoulders. "Here's a sample of what you get after you finish your plowing."

Moses gripped the plow and staggered forward. He'd seen the

scars on his cousin's back from the last time Cyrus had laid stripes on him. Tom had been in awful pain and unable to work for days.

Near the end of the day, the overseer ordered Tom to strip off Moses' shirt and tie his hands together around a tree.

"Be brave." Tom hurried away.

Cyrus swaggered over to check that all was ready. He pointed his whip at Tom and the others. "Everyone watch. You'll see what happens to lazy slackers."

The crack of the whip split the air. Moses screamed in agony, unable to keep silent because of the searing pain. The overseer kept adding stripe after stripe until Moses' bare back dripped with blood.

Moses swallowed a cry to Cyrus for mercy. He knew it was useless. *Oh, Lord, please! Keep Cyrus from killin' me like he kilt Mammy.*

Cyrus mopped his brow with a white handkerchief. He carefully wiped the blood from the whip. He called to Tom to come untie Moses' hands. As the setting sun blazed orange on the horizon, the overseer strode away.

Tom freed Moses' hands, grimacing at his cousin's back. Moses groaned and sank to the ground. "I hate him. I'm in mis'ry." His face twisted. "He'll get his whippin' on judgment day."

Aunt Bess ran to Moses and leaned over him. "Let's get you fixed up with soothin' herbs."

Moses tried to stand. "Cyrus be the devil and I hate him."

Uncle Otis, Tom's pappy, braced the boy as he staggered the half-mile back to the cabin. His aunt doctored his wounds, with Moses groaning in pain.

Tom stared at the blood oozing from the stripes on his cousin's back. "Maybe I be next."

When Grampa came home from the Big House, he clucked his tongue. "Moses sure to get hisself auctioned downriver next week. 'Less he runs off."

Aunt Bess frowned. "Don't be puttin' no ideas in his head."

"Your own sister be dead from whippin'." Grampa shook his head. "That overseer be the death of Moses. Runnin' off be the onliest way to stay alive."

Moses closed his eyes. *I be in this here place my whole life. But this place be a prison! Got to get loose. Tom and me got to run.*

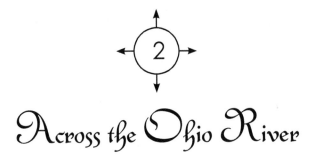

Across the Ohio River

John Parker's Foundry, Ripley, Ohio

Across the Ohio River from the farm where Moses and Tom slaved in the fields, the town of Ripley, Ohio, buzzed with industry. Outside the Ripley foundry, Will Butler leaned over and dug a pocketknife from the ground. Will already had a cheap knife in his pocket, as most sixteen-year-old boys did, but he'd never seen one this fancy. He wiped the knife on his pants and turned it over in his hands. *Whooee! Fine piece of work. Engraved eagle on the handle.*

His father peered over his shoulder. "What'd you find?" Will held it up. "Bet it cost a pretty penny. The man that lost it'll be glad to get it back."

Will's face fell. "Wish I could keep it."

His father gave him a long look and shook his head. "What if it was yours and you lost it?"

"You're right, Pa." Will sighed and turned the knife over again, rubbing the engraving. "I'll give it to Mr. Parker. He can ask the workers if they lost it. Maybe nobody will claim it. Then I can keep it, right?"

"Right. Now let's get in there and get to work." Both Will and his father worked for John Parker, a free black man who owned the foundry in Ripley.

As he waited with the knife, Will overheard a red-haired fellow-worker talking to Mr. Parker. "Hear about them three slaves what run off from Compton's farm? They stole a skiff and came ashore right by Front Street. Then they just disappeared."

Will shook his head. *Cutter is a loudmouth. Always complaining about Ripley citizens helping runaway slaves. His uncle owns slaves across the river in Kentucky.*

With a smirk, Cutter leaned toward Parker. "Don't suppose you know anything about it?"

Parker leaned his bulk toward Cutter. "If I did, I wouldn't tell you."

The man sneered, showing two jagged teeth. "You're on the wrong side of the Fugitive Slave Law, Parker. The U.S. Marshalls will catch you someday, and you'll end up in jail."

"If that happens, you'd be out of a job!" Parker folded his arms across his broad chest. "Now get to work, Cutter. Young Butler here has something worthwhile to ask me, I'll wager."

Cutter turned to Will and poked him in the chest. "Butler, you and your Pa live on Front Street, don't you? Better watch out! Some dark night them runaways will come knocking at your door."

Will clutched the knife in his hand and glanced across the room at his father. The idea of a runaway needing his help made the skin on his neck prickle. *Fugitive? Knocking at our door? Would we open it?*

When Cutter had gone to his workstation, Will held out the knife. "Um, Mr. Parker, I found this knife halfway buried in the ground out front. Pa says probably some worker lost it. But … "

"But you'd like to keep it?" Will nodded. Parker grinned and took the knife. "I appreciate your honesty. I'll say a knife's been found, but the owner has to describe it before he gets it back."

Will nodded and headed to his job for the day, packing finished parts into boxes and printing the addresses. All morning a question nagged the back of his mind. *Would we open our door to a fugitive?*

Everyone sat on logs outside at lunch. The men kept up a steady conversation about the weather, about the newest steamship on the Ohio, and about the vote in Kansas Territory. Will wished they'd talk about runaways.

As they walked home after work, Will asked his father the question he'd chewed on all day. The answer surprised him.

His father stopped short. "Would you like your pa in jail?"

"No! I'd have to take care of Ma and my sisters and brother. And earn enough to feed us all. No, I sure would not like it."

Pa started walking again. "The Fugitive Slave Law demands we help the slave catcher, not the slave."

"Then it's a bad law."

"But it's still the law. I'm not in favor of slavery, but I could go to jail for years and pay a thousand dollar fine if I helped even one runaway."

"But Mr. Parker does it. I heard he's helped many."

"He's smart enough not to hide them in his house. And so far, he hasn't been caught.

Pa pointed at the two-story house just ahead and dropped his voice. "See, there's Mr. McCague's house. He hides fugitives for Parker. But he owns a pork-packing factory so he could afford a thousand dollar fine."

"Mr. Cutter acts like he knows enough to get Mr. Parker or even Mr. McCague into trouble with this law." Will scratched his head.

Pa snorted. "Somehow Parker always makes the fugitives disappear. He's got a string of places he sends them."

"Right here in Ripley? "

"Yep. And stations all the way to Canada."

"Stations?"

"The stations are safe houses or barns. Even churches. They call them that because the fugitives move from one place to the next like a railroad. But it's secret, so it's called the Underground Railroad."

As they climbed their steps, Will sighed. "I hope I never have to turn away somebody who just wants his freedom."

As soon as he and Pa walked in the door, Will knew something was wrong. Their neat two-story house on Front Street usually bustled with kitchen noises as his mother fixed supper. Not this evening. Polly, his twelve-year-old sister, was crying on Ma's shoulder. Hope and Charity, his other younger sisters, and Jonah, his little brother, hung on Ma's skirt and whimpered.

"What happened?" Pa strode across the parlor and put his arm around his daughter.

Ma pulled a strand of hair out of her eyes and tucked it under her cap. "Polly was coming back two minutes ago from errands on Front Street. That evil man Rufus Cutter threatened her. Scared her half to death."

Pa frowned as he lifted Polly's chin. "What'd he say to you?"

"He called Mr. Parker awful names. He said anybody who's his friend is just as low-down as he is." Polly's plump cheeks were streaked with tears and her green eyes brimmed with more. "He said we better watch out, 'cause when they put Mr. Parker in jail, they'd run all his friends out of town." Polly put her face in her hands and continued to cry.

Pa patted her shoulder. "When I get my hands on him . . . " He clenched his fists.

Ma grabbed Pa's arm. "No! Fighting won't help. Cutter and his friends will beat you up."

Will frowned. "Polly, you shouldn't even listen to that man. He's just trying to stir up trouble."

Will had disliked Cutter from the first time he'd heard him sounding off against abolitionists and those who helped fugitives. Others at Parker's foundry agreed with Cutter, but at least they kept quiet about it.

Ma gave Polly a hankie for her tears and sent her to the kitchen to stir the stew. "Jonah, you get some kindling. Hope and Charity, finish setting the table. I need to speak with your father." When all but Will had gone, she bit her lip. "What shall we do, Henry?"

"You're right, I can't win a fight." Pa took off his hat and hung it on its peg. "Cutter is a blowhard. He sounds off because his brother is a city official, but it's mostly hot air. It'll be hard, but I'll try to ignore him."

Ma smoothed her apron and straightened her shoulders. "There are brave men in this town who take a moral stand against such as Rufus Cutter."

"Just who are you thinking of?"

"Reverend John Rankin and his church. I think we ought to start going there, regular."

Will glanced at the Bible on the shelf. "Pa, Mr. Adams next to me at the foundry says Reverend Rankin shows from the Bible how slavery's wrong."

Pa paced from the fireplace to the settee and back again. "I already know it's wrong, son, but the economy of the whole nation hinges on it."

Will thought for a minute. "I know about cotton. They grow it in the south, then steamboats carry it north where they make cloth out of it."

"Not just cotton. Rice, corn, tobacco, sugar cane." Pa waved his hand and kept pacing. "All of them depend on slave labor."

"God will judge our land for this evil." Ma wrung her hands.

"You make a good preacher, my dear. But you know it's too big for us to do anything about it."

Ma gave him a long look. "Other people are doing something about it all the time, Henry. Some day soon we may be needed to help someone seeking his freedom."

Will bit his lip. *That question again. Help a runaway? Even Pa and Ma can't agree. I don't know either.*

The Brush Arbor

Simon Anderson Farm, Maysville, Kentucky

Moses moaned throughout the night in spite of the salve of ground oak leaves Aunt Bess smoothed on his back. Next morning, he stayed back from working in the fields, quaking inside for fear Cyrus would come find him.

The following day, Sunday, no overseer blew a bugle blast to waken the slaves for their work in the fields. Yet the Lord's Day was hardly a day of rest, since all personal tasks must be done that day. Aunt Bess bustled outdoors to do the washing. Uncle Otis slung three traps over his shoulder and headed toward the woods.

Before Tom went out with his fishing pole, he knelt by his cousin. "You any better today?"

Moses moaned. "I'm hurtin' worse."

Tom rocked back on his heels. "Cyrus and the devil be like two peas in a pod."

Moses lifted himself up on one elbow. "I hate 'em both."

Aunt Bess came in then, shaking her head. "The Good Book say, hatin' be wrong. Better come to the preachin' at noon."

When the sun rose high in the sky, Moses dragged himself to the brush arbor. The singing of the others in this simple shelter would comfort his pain.

Grampa waved his arms, leading the music. "Sing with me, now! When Israel was in Egypt's land." Singing burst forth from the youngest to the oldest. Moses grinned, joining the rest as they clapped out the rhythm.

"Let my people go," the crowd sang. The children stomped their bare feet.

Grampa sang out, "Oppressed so hard they could not stand."

The chorus sounded like a mournful wail. "Let my people go. Go down, Moses. 'Way down in Egypt's land. Tell old Pharaoh. Let my people go."

Moses sang out the words. *We singin' my song. Lord, I want to be free.*

Trembling, an ancient black man with a white beard stood before the crowd. He brandished his Bible. "God Almighty love his black chillen just as much as his white ones. Some day, no more whippin's. And all our tribulation be done."

"Hallelujah! No more whippin's." Aunt Bess clapped her hands and smiled at Moses.

The preacher nodded and patted his Bible. "Someday we have shoes what fit our feet. We have all we want to eat and fresh meat, too."

Uncle Otis clapped his hands. "Amen, brother."

A chorus of 'Hallelujahs' and 'Praise the Lords' followed, from the youngest to the oldest. Moses raised his hands in prayer. *Lord, I want to be free.*

The old preacher lifted his Bible again. "You a slave to sin? Repent! You a slave to hate? Repent! Believe in Jesus. Jesus died for you. Now grab ahold on him."

"Preach it, brother." Grampa jumped to his feet and clapped his hands.

Calls of "Amen, brother" came from many in the crowd.

Moses closed his eyes and covered his face with his hands. *Oh Lord, I be a slave twice. I be a slave to sin and hate, just like the preacher say. I hate Cyrus for the whippin' what killed my mammy. I hate Cyrus for whippin' me.*

The preacher gazed at Moses. "Almighty God, your Spirit be workin'. Show this boy his sin. Open his eyes by your Spirit."

I be full of sin Lord. Take the hate away. Moses began to weep. He raised his eyes and called, "Lord, save me!"

The preacher waved his Bible and shouted, "Hallelujah! Angels in glory rejoicin' alongside this sinner. He repent, just like the Word say. He grab ahold on Jesus."

Grampa shook Moses' hand. "Now you be a child of God." He turned to the crowd. "Sing with me, now, 'Steal away, steal away, steal away to Jesus.'"

The congregation joined in, "Steal away, steal away home. I ain't got long to stay here."

"My Lord, He calls me, He calls me by the thunder." Grampa's voice boomed like thunder.

Moses heart overflowed with happiness and he joined the others to sing, "The trumpet sounds within-a my soul. I ain't got long to stay here."

"Green trees are a-bendin'. Poor sinner stand a-tremblin'." Grampa waved his arms like he was one of the trees.

More tears rolled down Moses' cheeks as he joined in singing. "The trumpet sounds within-a my soul. I ain't got long to stay here."

Moses glanced over at Tom and nodded. Tom knew. They'd run off soon.

After the worship time, Moses stopped by his mammy's grave to say goodbye. The rough board with her name scratched on it had nearly disappeared underneath the tall grass. He knelt beside it, pushed the grass aside, and poured out his heart.

"Ma, I got saved! Jesus got ahold of my heart. Me and Tom goin' to leave soon. Goin' for freedom."

Moses stood and looked at the plowed field nearby. "When I run off, I won't be comin' by here no more. But I won't forget you, Mammy. The one what taught me to do right. The one what learn me my letters and numbers. I make you proud, Mammy."

Rev. Rankin's Church

Ripley, Ohio

Dressed in their Sunday best, Will, Polly, Hope, Charity, and Jonah followed their parents down Front Street. They paraded down Mulberry Street and trooped up the steps of Reverend Rankin's Church. Neighbors greeted them, and the Butlers nodded back. Pa shepherded his family to a pew near the back.

Polly leaned around a lady with a fancy hat so she could see the family in the front pew. Will followed her gaze and counted twelve children seated beside a couple dressed in black. *That's probably the Rankin family. There's a boy my age.*

A song leader announced the first hymn, one the whole family knew well. Pa's bass voice boomed, "Rock of Ages, cleft for me. Let me hide myself in thee."

Will, Polly, and the other Butler children joined the singing. "Let the water and the blood, from thy wounded side which flowed, be of sin a double cure. Save from wrath, and make me pure."

This hymn was one of Will's favorites. *Jesus' death is the cure for sin. He'll keep us safe from the wrath of God. Ma taught me all about*

Jesus when I was little. Today I want to know about slavery. Does the Bible say anything about having slaves?

The preacher, a trim, clean-shaven man of about sixty, climbed into the pulpit and opened his large Bible.

Will glanced sideways at his father as Reverend Rankin began preaching. *This is just what I wanted to know.*

"The skin is but the dress which God has thrown over the human frame. As a kind father dresses out his daughters in white, red, olive, brown, and black, he counts them all alike as his children. So, the good Father of the Universe has dressed out his children in colors according to the various climates in which they dwell."

Pa's frowning. But that makes sense to me. Will leaned forward to hear what else this preacher would say.

"All are beautiful; why should they despise one another? It is a criticism of our Maker to judge our fellow men by the difference of their skin color. It is one of the blackest crimes of the human heart. It ought to be abolished." Reverend Rankin leaned forward and pointed. "It can be abolished. We must not turn a blind eye to the ones who need our help."

Will felt like Reverend Rankin pointed right at their family. He shifted in the pew.

Polly reached over and squeezed her brother's hand. He smiled. Whatever his parents decided, Will knew the answer to his nagging question. The black runaway needing help was just as much God's child as any other person. And he knew Polly felt the same way.

Polly and Will, leading the Butler family parade after church, whispered about the sermon as they walked home. Their parents, the last ones in line, discussed the minister's ideas out loud.

Pa shook his finger in the air. "No wonder people call that man a wild-eyed abolitionist. He tells us to break the law and put our money and property in danger."

"Henry, God's law is above man's law," Ma said.

Pa's voice rose a bit higher. "Listen, Hannah. The Bible says we're to obey the government."

"Even when the government's law forbids us to help one of God's children?"

"Right. Let's get this straight. I'm not going to jail and pay a thousand-dollar fine just to help somebody I don't even know." Pa smacked his fist into his palm. "No matter if he's black, brown, red, or white."

Ma looked out over the Ohio, sparkling in the sun. "Would you like me to make gravy for the pork roast today?" she asked.

Pa smiled, thinking he'd gotten the last word. "That would be very tasty, I'm sure. Just use a lighter hand with the pepper this time, please."

Will and Polly had stopped their whispering so they could hear what their parents said. Now Polly shook her head. "We better not ask Pa anything about the preacher's message."

"Better not ask him if we could help a runaway, either."

Polly gave her brother a sideways look. "If we never ask, then he won't tell us not to."

"You're pretty smart, for a girl!" Will smiled at his sister.

Ready, Set...

Simon Anderson Farm, Maysville, Kentucky

Aunt Bess doctored Moses Monday morning and evening. He still had plenty of pain, but the scabs weren't oozing any more.

When Tom came home, he told Moses, "Cyrus he snarl all the livelong day. He say, 'that worthless boy better be here, dawn tomorrow to finish the plowin'. Even if I have to drag him behind the mule.'"

"Better get to the fields tomorrow." Uncle Otis shook his finger at Moses.

Moses shook his head. "My back's still painin' me somethin' fierce."

Uncle Otis crossed his arms. "You be there, or I be the one draggin', not the mule."

"Cyrus be to blame," Moses moaned. "That whippin' be why I ain't workin'. It done broke my poor back."

"You be on Cyrus' auction list. Just four days from now. We better run afore that," Tom said.

Moses sat up. "Just thinkin' on runnin' give my legs the wobbles."

"It be worse to stay than run." Grampa's brow was creased with worry.

Tom strode over to the wall and grabbed a burlap sack. "We got to get ready. Mammy, bake some corn pone, and--"

"Whoa, boy." Grampa hung the sack in its place. "This be the plan." He sat beside Moses and motioned Tom to join them. "three nights from now, you boys meet up with a fellow by the name John Parker. I send word and he send back. He bringin' a skiff to the Kentucky side and takin' you both across the Ohio."

"How we suppose to figure out where to meet this John Parker?" Moses asked.

Grampa took a stick and scratched a map in the dirt. "Follow the drinkin' gourd stars, they point north. This here be Master Simon's farm. Next be the woods. Next the Maysville Road. Other side of it be the Ohio."

Tom leaned forward. "Draw on the other roads."

Grampa whacked the stick on the ground. "No. Stay off the roads. Walk zig zags." He drew lines like bent snakes. "Walk through the streams to keep the hounds from smellin' you. Them dogs'll eat you alive."

Moses stomach turned over. "They be dogs to worry us? If we steal away at night, nobody miss us till next mornin'."

"The night patrollers have dogs. So stay away from the roads. Dogs find your smell, you're done gone." Grampa shook his head. "Them hounds be death for runaways."

Moses pointed to the map. "At the river, how do Mr. Parker find us in the dark?"

"Good boy. Plannin' ahead already. You be the leader," Grampa said.

He drew the Ohio River in the dirt. "The Ohio flow west for a mile or two past Maysville, here. Then it flow north for about three mile. When it change back to goin' west, then look around. There's a spot with a storm-broke tree. Points downriver. When you see that tree, then look for Mr. Parker."

Moses scratched his head. "He a black man?"

"Yep, a big strong one. He use to be a slave hisself. He got connections."

Tom groaned. "Too much to remember."

"You ain't scared?" Moses wagged his finger at Tom.

Grampa rubbed out the map with his foot and gave the stick to Tom. "Now you draw it."

Tom frowned, but began to draw. Moses helped him, adding details.

Grampa nodded and smiled. "That's it. Start out after dark. Journey about five mile to the meetin' spot at the storm-broke tree. Wait in the dark till Mr. Parker come across in the skiff." The old man pointed his bony finger at Moses, then at Tom. "You boys stick together. Use both your heads. Moses can't be leader 'less he have a follower."

Moses pointed at Tom. "See, you got to go where I say."

Tom rolled his eyes.

Moses struggled to his feet to peer at the sky. "There be the drinkin' gourd, pointin' the way. And the moon. It be smilin' at us, I declare. God be likin' our plan."

Grampa wagged his finger at them. "The devil be hearin' these plans. Bible say, he be a roarin' lion, ready to eat you up!" The old man folded his hands and closed his eyes. "But we all be a-prayin'."

Will's New Job

John Parker's Foundry, Ripley, Ohio

Two days later, Will followed Pa into the foundry and Mr. Parker motioned to him. He handed Will the engraved pocketknife. "Nobody claimed this. It's yours."

Will's grin nearly split his face. "Thank you, sir!" He slid it into his pocket before his boss changed his mind.

Rufus Cutter strode past. "That man's looking for trouble," Mr. Parker said.

Will nodded. "He even threatened my sister Polly one afternoon last week. She got real upset when he told her we'd get run out of town because we're friends with you."

Parker gave Will a keen look. He lowered his voice. "Are you a friend to fugitives?"

Will nodded slowly. "We heard Reverend Rankin preach on Sunday. Polly and me are decided on that score. But not Pa."

Parker lowered his voice to a bare whisper. "I got word that two boys from near Maysville are heading north Thursday night. I need a link in the chain of helping hands."

Will's eyes widened. "I'll help. But I can't speak for Polly."

"I'll give you details tomorrow." Parker turned to oversee the loading of a shipment onto a waiting wagon.

Will hustled to his work area, with questions swirling through his mind. *Thursday night. What will I do? Sneak out without parents knowing? Go against Pa? Get caught and go to jail?*

On the way home from work, Will showed his new knife to his father, but said nothing about the rest of his conversation with Mr. Parker. His father never brought up the subject of Reverend Rankin's sermon, so Will figured it was best not to talk about it.

At work the following day, Mr. Parker gave Will an outdoor job, packing the wagon full of foundry products for the steamship. Later, Mr. Parker came to check on progress. "Are you sure you want to get mixed up with helping runaways? It might be dangerous."

"So I've heard. But I'm ready." Will kept packing the boxes.

"Tomorrow night I'll bring those boys to this side of the Ohio." Mr. Parker lifted a box into the back of the wagon. "Meet me at Three Mile Creek. You know where that is?"

"Yep. Upriver about three miles from Ripley."

"I'll deliver the boys around two or three in the morning. You lead them through the underbrush to Ripley. Then up the hundred stone steps to John Rankin's house."

"What should I watch out for? You said it was dangerous." Will stayed busy. That way if anybody was watching they wouldn't suspect a thing.

"Ripley is crawling with slave catchers looking for a fast dollar. At dawn, the federal marshals start roaming the streets. There are people like Cutter who will turn you in out of meanness and to get the reward for the boys."

"A reward right off?"

"A reward, mark my words. The monthly auction at the

courthouse in Maysville is Friday. A strong, healthy young male brings maybe $1,800.00, maybe more."

Parker started to leave, then turned back. "Keep all this under your hat."

Will nodded and went back to work. The details repeated themselves in his mind as if he were afraid he might forget them. *Thursday night. Two in the morning. Three Mile Creek. Climb the steps to Rankin's house.*

As he walked home with Pa, Will tried to act normal. He let Pa do most of the talking, so no hint of his plans would slip into the conversation.

Pa asked him for help in spading up their garden for the early crops. "Your ma depends on the cabbage to keep us in kraut all winter."

"Polly likes to plant her flowers near the house. I'll spade up that part, too," Will said.

"She'll probably bake you a pie to show her appreciation."

"And Ma can thank us both if she makes a sauerkraut cake." Will laughed out loud.

Will and Pa started digging as soon as they got home. When Will began on Polly's garden plot, she came out to give directions. "How did your day go, Will?"

"About the same as usual." Will shrugged and kept spading.

Polly dropped her voice. "I overheard something at the dry goods store you should know."

Will stopped spading.

"Keep digging like nothing's different," said Polly.

When Will went back to spading, Polly continued, "Miz Cutter was saying something about a raid. Tomorrow night a bunch of men are headed to the Rankins'."

"That's awful!" Will forgot to stay quiet.

"Shh!"

"Don't you think we ought to tell Pa? Or at least warn Reverend Rankin?"

Polly looked over at her father, spading the main plot. "Well, Pa acted like he didn't care for Reverend Rankin's extreme stand against slavery, so I didn't want to say anything."

"The Rankins need to be warned." Will began to spade as if there were buried treasure under the flowerbed and then turned to Polly. "Can you keep a secret?"

"Of course."

"Tomorrow night I'm helping Mr. Parker by taking some fugitives up to the Rankin house."

Polly's mouth dropped open. "Then that means it won't be safe." Her face turned pale. "If Cutter and his friends surround the Rankin's house, someone could get killed."

"Right. I'll ask Mr. Parker to warn them and send us to another station."

Pa finished spading the vegetable garden and put away his shovel. "Polly, did your brother do a good job getting this plot ready for your flower seeds?"

"He did a fine job."

Will grinned at his sister. "Pa said you'd pay me with a pie. I saw the rhubarb behind the shed, ready to pick."

Polly planted her hands on her hips. "Go pick it and you shall have your pie."

Will stashed his shovel in the shed and went to pull the rhubarb. He looked toward the top of the hill behind Ripley. Dusk brought shadows to the staghorn sumacs on the hill, but the sun still reflected from the lone house at the top. Will caught his breath. Someone lit a candle in a window. *The Rankin House. The candle lights the way to freedom.*

One More Day

Simon Anderson Farm, Maysville, Kentucky

Moses worked in the fields, but he didn't dare let on how bad he hurt. Cyrus watched him all day like he hoped to catch him doing something to earn another whipping.

As they plodded back to the cabin, Moses chattered about their plans. Tom lagged behind, so Moses asked, "You changin' your mind about runnin' away?"

"Never see my mammy and pappy again, for sure."

"We come back and help the whole family. When we be free."

That night Aunt Bess mixed tears with the salve she spread on Moses' back. "Never see you boys again. But runnin' be the only way to be free."

Next morning Grampa drew the map in the dirt one more time before he left for the Big House. "Let's pray the Lord to watch over you boys." He put his hands on their heads and prayed them a blessing. "Remember to ask the Lord to guide you."

Aunt Bess handed Moses a sack full of corn pone to carry and Uncle Otis gave Tom a pocketknife.

Moses moved a little faster to the field than the day before. "Today my last day. Cyrus-devil cain't rile me no more about workin' too slow." He carried the food sack under his shirt and hid it in the tall grass. *Dark cain't come too soon. Goodbye Cyrus-devil, hello freedom.*

Cyrus met them with an evil smile. He pointed to a wagon loaded with sacks of seed corn. "See all that corn? Today you work hard and fast and get it all planted. Or else you're working all night, by the light of the moon. A change in the weather's coming, and we want the rain to water the seeds."

The field hands clutched planting sacks. After they had filled them, Cyrus lined them up along the top edge of the field, spaced four rows apart. "Start there and do four furrows each. We'll make this a game. The first one done gets to eat lunch. The rest of you can eat when your rows are done, unless the mule with the food and water has already gone back to the barn."

Moses winced as he put the heavy sack across his throbbing shoulder. *Them furrows be a mile each. Plant fast as I can. Got to get done. Won't get no food and no water.*

The sun shone behind a haze of humid air, beating down on the workers. Cyrus leaned against a tree, watching the slow and the weak like a buzzard.

Aunt Bess couldn't carry both Tillie and a planting sack at the same time, so she put the baby in the grass near her first furrow. Toward noon the baby began to squall.

Cyrus cracked his whip toward Aunt Bess. "Shut up that yowling brat, or I'll shut her up for you."

She hurried to pick up Tillie and quieted her with soothing words. She strapped the baby on her back and picked up the planting sack again. She worked too slowly for Cyrus, who screamed insults at her.

The mule with the food and water arrived at lunchtime. Every worker licked parched lips, yet kept planting. Cyrus sat in the shade to enjoy his lunch, the only one who ate or drank. Even Uncle Otis was scarcely half done with his allotment. He bent down, trying to plant even faster. Moses had kept pace with Tom at first, but now lagged far behind.

Tom whispered to his cousin when he had a chance. "We be in trouble if we miss Mr. Parker and the boat."

"Cain't go any faster," Moses said.

By late in the afternoon, five field hands had finished their four furrows and earned food and water. Two of them, Tom and Uncle Otis, had the same idea—they stashed extra cornbread inside their shirts to share with others. About half the workers got their furrows finished by sundown. That was too late for lunch and water, since the mule and wagon had left hours before.

Cyrus lit several lanterns as dusk grew to darkness. He shouted, "Work faster or I'll whip your lazy bones." The fastest workers helped the others finish their rows.

Moses grew restless. *Lord, help us. Be hours afore we be done plantin'. What happen to me and Tom if we miss our boat ride?*

When the last row was planted. Cyrus grabbed his whip and his lantern and disappeared down the lane. Everyone flopped on the grass, too weary to take a step toward home, food, and water.

After he collected the hidden sack from the edge of the field, Moses sank to the ground next to Tom. "Look at that moon, high already. Rest a spell, then you and me take to the woods."

Tom leaned back to look in the sky. "Look. A ring around the moon."

Moses craned his neck to see. "Red ring around the moon, mean it rain soon."

"But where be the stars?"

"They be gone."

"Which way we go?"

"Your pappy will know." He pulled Tom up. "C'mon. You ain't losin' your nerve?"

"Shut up."

Uncle Otis looked at the sky and shook his head. "If you cain't see the stars, follow the stream. It flow to the big river. In the woods, look at tree moss. It grow thicker on the north side."

"Start us off right from here," Moses said.

Uncle Otis pointed past the plowed and planted field to the thick woods beyond. "That be north." He folded his hands and held them high. "We be a-prayin'."

Moses strode toward the woods.

Tom took a few steps and turned to wave goodbye to his pappy. "Tell Mammy I love her."

Moses swallowed the big lump in his throat. *I be leavin' my mammy, too. Mammy, I learn to read. I come back. And bring the whole family to freedom.*

The boys disappeared into the woods, heading north.

Change of Plans

John Parker's Foundry, Ripley, Ohio

Will worried all night long about the raid Polly had heard Miz Cutter talk about. He would ask Mr. Parker to warn Reverend Rankin, saying nothing to Pa.

As he walked to work with Pa, Will tried to act relaxed. "Look at the haze hanging over the river. I'd guess it'll rain by tomorrow." *Hope it holds off. May get soaked.*

"Yep. Good thing we got the garden spaded so Ma and Polly can get their seeds planted."

A knot of men huddled in front of the foundry like they were plotting something secret. When they noticed Will and Pa they hurried inside, with Cutter leading the way.

Will's stomach did a flip-flop. *Maybe I should tell Pa what Polly heard. Hate to keep secrets from Pa.*

Shouts from the foundry interrupted Will's thoughts. Inside, Cutter was scuffling with a stocky man with bulging muscles.

"What's going on here?" Parker asked.

The stocky man stepped back and pointed at Cutter. "He threatened me. He said—"

Cutter, reaching for the knife in his belt, sprang toward the man. "Keep your mouth shut or else."

"Hold it, Cutter." Parker forced his burly frame between the two and pushed Cutter back. "Get to work. And no more brawling. Or you'll both be out of a job."

Will walked to his work area trying to guess what the tussle was about. *Cutter had threatened the man. 'Go on the raid tonight, or something bad would happen?' Something bad might happen to me, too.*

When he had a chance, Will told Mr. Parker about Cutter's planned raid on the Rankin's house. Parker shook his head. "That changes things. I'll have to warn him."

"And I shouldn't go there, right?"

Parker nodded, scratching his head in thought. "I'll ask Thomas Collins to let you hide in his cabinet shop. It's right on Front Street, not far from your house. You know where it is?"

"Yes, we bought a table from him once. I've even been in his shop."

"Careful no one's around when you sneak in. If anyone comes to the shop, hide inside the coffins."

"Coffins?" Will shuddered. *Better make sure I'm right with God before I climb into one of those.*

"Two fugitives and I escaped a gang of slave catchers one night by hiding in Collins' coffins." Parker chuckled. "I tell you, my heart was thumping. I got out of that death-box as soon as the gang left."

"Maybe the slave catchers were scared, too," Will said.

"Could be. Lots of superstitious people around here."

"So, I'm supposed to meet you and the two boys at Three Mile Creek around two in the morning?"

Parker nodded and turned to go. "You may be waiting a long time, so don't give up."

"I won't." Will bent his head to his work again. *At least I think I'll be there.*

After work, Will walked home with his father and chatted about nothing of importance.

He played catch with Jonah and ate dinner with his family. Ma counted off the kinds of seeds she'd planted.

After dinner, Polly marched from the kitchen and presented Will with his rhubarb pie.

Will grabbed his fork and took a bite. "This rhubarb pie is the best I've had all year."

Polly beamed.

"Of course it's the only one I've had all year." Will teased his sister.

Later, Polly gave him a searching look, but asked no questions.

Will said goodnight, went to his room, and undressed for bed. *Whew, Pa and Ma don't suspect a thing. Jonah's asleep. He's angelic when he's asleep.*

Will listened to the mantel clock chime. At half past eleven he climbed out of bed and got dressed. He patted his pocket to make sure his new knife was there. He pushed the door open a crack and stopped short. The glow of a candle shone from the kitchen and he heard his parents talking softly. His father's voice carried up the stairs and Will caught a few words. "Cutter. Rankin. Tonight."

Will's jaw dropped. *Does Pa know about the raid? Maybe he's going to join Cutter. Or is he going to help the Rankins? Pa could be in danger either way. Cutter has both a knife and a gun.* Will stood behind the door, listening and wondering what to do.

Will heard the back door open and close. *Pa's gone.*

He heard his mother's light step on the stairs just in time to pull his door closed. After his mother's bedroom door closed, Will crept downstairs. *Pa's gun's gone from the pegs where it belongs. He must be expecting trouble.*

The moon, high in the sky, shone through a reddish ring. Will shivered in the damp air. *Lord, watch over Pa. Lord, am I doing the right thing? I'll walk fast. Should take about an hour to Three Mile Creek.*

Will stayed in the shadows, heading east.

9

Howling and Growling

Near Maysville, Kentucky

Moses and Tom plunged into the trees, sticking close together. They fought their way through briers and saplings, and headed north.

Tom stumbled over a root. "Mose, slow down." He leaned against a tree. "I be hungry. And thirsty."

"We got to keep on." Moses handed Tom a corn pone from the sack. "You can get a drink at the stream. Should be soon. Now, c'mon."

They struggled on, past tangled grapevines and scratchy briars. On their bellies by the stream, they slurped as much water as they could hold.

Something howled deep in the woods. Tom's eyes grew large and he shivered. "Hear that noise?"

"Hounds! Get in the water. Wash off your smell." They ran through the shallows and waded in up to their waists. The baying came again, louder and longer. Then it stopped.

"Grampa say they eat us alive!" Tom tried to hurry, but stumbled and fell forward against Moses.

The boys plunged ahead until the water came up to their chests. They struggled to walk through the middle of the stream and the howling began again. It came from their left, so they climbed up the opposite bank.

"That devil Cyrus. He sic the hounds on us!" Tom hunted for a heavy stick.

The howling changed to a crying whimper. Moses tilted his head. "The sound be a-comin' from the same place, not gettin' closer."

"Too close for me."

"Sounds like cryin', like the hound be hurt. Let's go see."

"You crazy? I'm stayin' here." Tom sat down. "Anyhow, I need a rest."

"Hand over the knife then."

"Pa gave it to me." Tom clutched his pocket.

"But I need it." Moses frowned. "C'mon. Give the knife."

"Stay here, then."

Moses lunged toward his cousin. "Give the knife. We ain't got much time."

Tom dug it out of his pocket and threw it on the ground. "Don't go bringin' no dog back here."

Moses felt in the dark for the knife. *Tom just bein' biggity. He be scared of dogs. Got bit once. I always want a pet dog.*

As he crossed the stream again, the whimpering sounds got louder. *It sound like just one dog. Not Cyrus' pack of hounds.*

He crept up close to a blackberry thicket before he saw the mangy yellow dog. *Somebody's pet. Poor dog. One ear bent down. Rope all tangled.*

Moses spoke soothing words as he advanced.

"Poor puppy. You all tangled." The dog whimpered, as if it understood Moses wanted to help.

The little dog had a bad cut on one front paw and a rope around its neck. A tangle of branches had captured the knotted end of the rope. Moses worked it loose with the knife, chatting with the dog all the while. "Tom and me done run away, too. Your master cruel? Now you be free."

The dog wagged its tail and licked Moses' hand.

Moses returned with his pet to Tom. "The Lord, he send us a dog."

"Not me. Send him back." Tom stopped chewing the corn pone and stared.

"He be my pet dog. He can guard us."

"Will he bite?"

Moses laughed. "He be friendly." As if to prove it, the dog tilted its head and wagged its tail at Tom.

Tom tossed his last bite of corn pone to the dog. "Maybe he be hungry." Before it hit the ground, the mangy animal snapped it up.

"You can name him."

"He got yeller fur. Cornpone be a good name."

The two boys walked through the shallows of the stream so the dog's paw would get washed. The quiet splash of water over rocks helped them find their way in the dark.

The dog limped behind at first, but soon strutted in front like an advance guard. They'd been walking for a while when Cornpone stopped, growling deep in his throat.

Moses leaned down to see the dog in the dim light. "Cornpone's back fur, it be a-standin' straight up like a brush." Moses felt shivers go down his own back.

Tom stopped, turning his head to hear. "Listen! Screams from somethin' big."

Moses listened, too. The night sounds of the woods and the splashing of the stream had surrounded them for the last hour. Now a screeching noise ripped the air in the dark woods.

Moses clutched his stomach. "It be a fierce animal. Lord, help us!"

←—○—→

RIPLEY, OHIO

Will made his way through the dark streets of Ripley toward the place he would meet Mr. Parker. *There's Mr. Collin's house and Mr. McCague's house. Those men take a big risk helping runaways.* He scrambled down the hill from Front Street toward the river. *Am I doing the right thing? Easier to hide down here. Plenty of bushes. Looks deserted.*

Near the edge of town he heard men's voices. *Rowdy. Probably drunk.*

He crept to a spot where he could see the street yet stay out of sight behind bushes. A cluster of five men, one with a lantern, marched down the middle of the street. They called out to a sixth man to catch up with them.

Will swallowed a gulp as he recognized the man with the lantern. *Cutter! All carrying guns. Lord, protect the Rankin family.*

He strained to recognize the other men, but it was too dark. *Is Pa in that crowd, or did he go to the Rankin's? Lord, protect him, too. And me.*

He watched until the men turned on a side street and headed up the hill behind the town. Then he hurried on his way. Worry twisted his insides. *The Rankins better have their doors locked and their guns ready. Good thing that preacher has grown sons. God will protect him.*

After he left Ripley, he braved hiking on the road. *Good, nobody's out tonight.* He smiled up at the moon. *I hope the rain holds off at least till morning.*

After hiking for a good while, he stopped short. The road dipped into a stream where stones made a shallow crossing. *Three Mile Creek. The meeting spot.*

He turned right and climbed down the bank toward the Ohio. It shimmered in the pale moonlight. On the shore, he found a tangle of driftwood logs. *I'm here plenty early. These branches make a decent chair. Clear view of anyone coming here by boat.*

As he waited, he wondered about the raid at the Rankins'. *I hope Pa went there to help. That would mean he's changed his mind. These raids against the law? Mr. Parker'll know. Bet Mr. Parker's house gets raided, too.*

He closed his eyes to rest them for a while, and fell asleep.

10

A Roaring Lion

Near Maysville, Kentucky

Moses and Tom took their cue from Cornpone, who continued to growl. Whatever was screaming and snarling off in the distance was dangerous.

Moses' voice quivered. "Get big sticks."

"It be the lion-devil! Grampa warn us about the lion eatin' us up." Tom grabbed his stick with both hands.

Cornpone's growling grew louder and more frenzied.

Moses gripped his club and tried to keep his knees from knocking together. *Lord, keep the beast from eatin' us up. Please, Lord.*

The unseen creature's snarling changed into a scream.

Tom grabbed fist-sized rocks from the bank of the stream. Moses ran to hunt his own supply.

The snarls and screams got louder and closer, and Cornpone reacted with frenzied barking.

Tom's eyes grew large and he nearly choked. "Maybe it be…a… c-catamount. P-Pa told me about them once. They creep close and leap on your back."

"That wildcat cain't sneak up on us. We got a dog, even if he ain't a very big dog." Moses strained to peer into the darkness.

"A big catamount might eat him first, then come after us." Tom readied his biggest rock.

Cornpone's barking geared to a feverish pitch. A streak of fur rushed toward them.

Tom shrieked and hurled his rock. It missed.

Cornpone raced toward the wildcat, braced his feet, and barked. The animal bared its fangs and crouched, as if waiting to pounce.

Moses threw a rock. Closer than Tom's, but still a miss.

The cat's eyes glowed in the dim moonlight. It leaped toward Cornpone. Its claws slashed at the dog, again and again. Cornpone, bleeding, backed off, but kept barking.

"Stay back, Cornpone!" Moses lobbed another rock at the animal. "Got him!"

The boys kept throwing rocks until they ran out of ammunition. The animal slunk into the shadows, waiting its chance to attack again.

"Throw sticks till I get more rocks!" Tom ran to the stream bank.

Moses advanced a few steps and threw his club-stick. He missed the cat by a few inches.

Tom threw a big rock and hit the wildcat in the side of the head. "I got him!" The cat turned and ran. Cornpone chased after him.

Moses ran and caught the dog's rope. "Stop! Stay here with us."

Tom collapsed on the ground. "Never seed such a brave dog! That catamount be twice as big as him."

Moses flopped beside him. "Sit, Cornpone." He studied the bloody gashes on the dog's side. "That catamount hurt our dog."

"But it didn't hurt us." Tom patted the dog's head.

"Praise the Lord! That wildcat be the most scary varmint I ever did see."

Tom tried to stand, but sank back down. "My legs so wobbly,

like I done run all the way home from the fields."

After a struggle, Moses stood. "We got to keep a-goin' or we miss findin' Mr. Parker."

"North. Which way?"

Moses pointed to the water beside them. "See, it be flowin' toward the Ohio."

He picked up their burlap bag and headed down the stream. Tom and the dog followed. They marched forward, though they could see only three steps ahead.

As the night wore on, Cornpone slowed down and Tom stumbled more and more often. "Ready for another rest, Mose."

"Not yet. We almost through the woods." Moses pointed ahead to a dim glow beyond the underbrush.

Cornpone scampered ahead and disappeared. Moses hurried after him. Tom gave a low moan and pushed forward. All three came out of the woods beside a road. Beyond the road they caught a glimpse of moonlight reflected on water.

"The Ohio!" Moses looked up. "Thanky, Lord."

Ohio River at Three Mile Creek

Will woke with a start to feel a chill breeze in his face. Dark clouds hid the moon. He stretched and stood. *How long did I sleep? Don't see anyone coming. Hope Mr. Parker hasn't come across already. Nothing to do but wait. Rain's coming soon. Sooner than Mr. Parker.*

He circled the tangle of driftwood and hunted until he found a spot under the largest log. *Good place to hide if I need it. From the rain or from slave catchers.*

He rubbed his eyes. *Don't want to sleep again. When will they come? How long have I been waiting? Two or three hours? Mr. Parker must be delayed. He should be here by now.*

Far-off screeches and hoots floated toward him on the night

breeze. *Owls. Wonder what makes those splashes along the shore.*

Will heard sounds from the road. *Men talking. Slave catchers watching the shore? How can I warn Mr. Parker not to come here?*

A gunshot split the air. Will's heart jumped into his throat, and he dove under the jumble of logs. He stared out the small opening facing the river. *The shot came from the road behind me. Were they shooting at me?*

A quiet rain began, making the night even darker. The men were silent and there were no more shots. *Maybe they're setting an ambush at the road. Of course. If they were down here, Mr. Parker wouldn't land the boat.*

Shivering, Will hunched down in his log hideaway. Drips landed on his neck and slid down his back. *Nothing to do but wait.*

11

Meeting on the River

Ohio River, near Maysville

Moses and Tom followed the shore of the Ohio, going downstream. Cornpone kept his nose to the ground, sniffing. Clouds scudded across the moon. The boys plodded ahead, their heads bent into the rain.

"Cain't see the t'other side, nohow," Tom said.

"We be lookin' for a storm-broke tree, this side."

The boys examined every tree and saw several with a paper fluttering in the breeze.

Tom ripped one down. "What these papers sayin'?"

"Probably tell somethin' important. That's a A." Moses pointed to all five A's on the paper. "Someday I kin read."

They walked farther, picking their way around drift-logs and rocks. Tom noticed the river bend toward the north. "What'd Grampa say? The Ohio flow north for three mile."

"Then it bend again to the west at the storm-broke tree." Moses tried to walk faster. "We got three mile of walkin' to do."

Before they'd walked a mile, Cornpone lifted his head and growled.

Tom halted, but he couldn't keep his body from shaking. "It ain't another catamount, is it?"

Moses, first in line, stopped short, nearly running into a large man whose dark shape seemed to appear from nowhere. "You be Mr. Parker?" He grabbed Cornpone's rope. "Hush, dog."

"And you're the boys needing a ride across the Ohio?" Mr. Parker's easy greeting made Moses wonder if he did this all the time.

"Yessir." Moses and Tom answered at the same time.

"Let me see the paper in your hand."

Tom handed him the damp sheet. "All on the way, these papers be on the trees."

"It's a reward poster." Parker grimaced and held the paper closer to read it. "But it's not offering money for runaways. Wanted, Dead or Alive. John Parker. $1,000 reward."

Moses' jaw dropped. "That be a heap of money."

Parker shrugged and tucked the paper in his shirt. "The skiff's downriver, but the dog can't go along. Too dangerous if it started to bark."

"Cornpone ain't really our dog," Tom said.

"We got him loose from a rope-tangle, then he rescue us from a catamount," Moses said.

Parker nodded. "Still a few big cats left in the deep woods. You're lucky you weren't his dinner."

"The Lord, he keep us safe." Moses grabbed Cornpone's rope.

"Tie him here so he won't follow us."

"C'mon, Cornpone, let's get you tied." Moses patted the dog and tied him to a nearby bush. "Bye, Cornpone. Some boy find hisself a good dog." He gave him a farewell hug.

The dog tugged at the rope, whimpered, and sat down to watch Moses leave.

Mr. Parker and Tom had a head start hiking toward the skiff, so Moses ran to catch up.

"Listen carefully, boys." Mr. Parker slowed just a little so they could hear every word. "Both of you must obey me, whatever I tell you to do. Neither one can cry out in fear or pain from now on. One shout could endanger us all."

"Yessir." They nodded.

"We'll row across the river and meet someone who'll take you to a safe place. You'll do just as he says, same as if I were telling you."

"Yessir. We will."

They hiked on in silence until they came to the skiff. Mr. Parker pointed to the front, and they both climbed in and lay in the bottom of the boat. He pushed off with the oar and then wrapped a rag around the oarlocks to muffle the sound.

Moses closed his eyes. *Oh, Lord, This be the Jordan and I be crossin' to freedom. Thanky, Lord.*

The slap of the water against the front of the boat lulled the boys to sleep. Moses fought the catamount and ran from a pack of dogs in his restless nap. The light rain obscured the shore until the skiff came within a few yards.

Moses woke with a start and raised himself to see what freedom looked like. *Just bushes and trees and rocks and mud. Ain't no different from Kentucky.*

He shook his cousin's shoulder. "Tom, we near to shore. Wake up. That land be free."

"Ohio's a free state, but plenty of people want to haul you back to Kentucky. Don't count yourself free till you're all the way to Canada," Mr. Parker said.

"Canada be a long long way." Moses slumped back down beside Tom.

Three Mile Creek, near Ripley, Ohio

Will hunkered down in his drift-log shelter. His homespun

shirt, smeared with mud, clung to his chest. *Won't be able to keep this night a secret from Ma. Must've been an hour since I heard that shot.*

He raised his eye to the opening and scanned the river for the hundredth time. He blinked to make sure he saw what he saw. A dark spot moved toward the Ohio shore. *Hope it's Parker. Won't leave cover till they get closer. Bet those men are still watching for him, too.*

After a few minutes, the dark spot took shape, a skiff with a man in it. Will shivered. *Is it Parker? Where are the boys? Must be someone else.*

He watched as the man brought the skiff to shore and climbed out, holding the rope and looking around. Two dark figures climbed ashore behind him.

Will ducked out from the drift-logs and ran toward the three figures. He looked back to see if anyone followed him. It was too dark to see, but he heard no footsteps. When he got closer, he shook his head in warning. "Mr. Parker. Some men are waiting to ambush you up on the road."

Mr. Parker turned and motioned the boys back into the boat. "We'll need to find a different landing spot. Climb in, Will."

Will waded out and clambered into the front with the boys. They looked scared, so Will smiled at them. "Don't say anything. Keep your heads down."

Mr. Parker rowed out to the middle where the current added to his speed. "You think there's a trap?"

"About an hour ago, I heard a gunshot and men's voices. It's been quiet since then, and I've stayed hidden," Will said.

"You spoiled their welcoming party. They may be aiming to collect the reward for me, dead or alive."

Will gulped. "Y-you? D-dead or alive?"

"They probably would prefer me dead. I'm too much trouble alive." Mr. Parker kept rowing the little skiff, lost in a misty world of its own.

Will shivered, pitying the boys huddled together to stay warm. *They can't be much older than Polly. And they just want to be free. I would, too.*

Mr. Parker leaned toward Will. "This rain hides us from spying eyes. In a few minutes we'll land in a cove a mile or so below Ripley. From there, you lead the boys to Collins' cabinet shop."

"Hope there won't be another welcoming party," Will said.

Mr. Parker raised his eyebrows. "The slave catchers will probably be watching my house, not Collins' shop."

Parker guided the skiff close to the shore. A tangle of trees grew close to the water, a perfect hiding place for the bounty hunters. As the moon came out from behind a cloud, the dark shapes shifted and Will's heart leaped to his throat.

Parker motioned for all of them to climb ashore. "The west edge of Ripley is a half mile from here. Follow the trail through the woods till you're across from Collins' place. Then watch for the right time to run across Front Street and hide in his shop building. He's all set with blankets and food for these boys."

"You ready for a hike?" Will put his arm around the two shivering beside him. *Wonder if they're as scared as I am.*

"Don't like the look of them woods." Moses tried to see into the darkness.

"Any catamounts in there?" Tom asked, gulping.

Will shook his head. "Not lately. Been three years since some hunters killed a wildcat near Ripley."

"Be on your way, Will. Dawn comes in about an hour. You should be back home before then," Mr. Parker said.

Will and the two freedom-seekers melted into the shadows.

Pine Coffins

Ripley, Ohio

In single file, the three boys slipped and slid on the trail through the woods. Raindrops dripped from the trees.

Moses' mind focused on following the young man ahead. *Will, Mr. Parker call him. Just keep goin'. I be so tired my bones be ready to fall in a heap. Put one foot in front of the other.*

He turned to see how Tom fared. Tom's eyes were closed and he was close to tumbling down the ridge of the trail. "Tom, wake up!"

"Unh! We there yet?" Tom opened his eyes and stopped short.

Moses caught a movement behind Tom. "Look out! Some creature's followin' us." Moses grabbed a rock and raised his arm to throw it.

The shadow moved closer and whimpered.

"Wait! Ain't that Cornpone?" Tom yanked Moses' arm down.

Will turned back and hissed, "What's going on?"

"Our dog found us again," Moses said.

"Cornpone save us from a catamount." Tom grinned and called the dog.

"But Mr. Parker make me tie him up before we cross in the boat," said Moses.

Cornpone limped and his cuts oozed. Tom grabbed his rope. "Poor dog be drippin' wet."

Will frowned. "He can't stay with you. He might give away your hiding place at Mr. Collins' shop."

"Yessir," Moses said.

Will thought a while. "I'll tie him up outside the shop. He can be a watchdog."

The boys hurried forward on the slippery trail. When the woods thinned to straggly saplings and bushes, Will crouched before moving forward. "Keep low."

As they hunkered in the underbrush, a horse-drawn wagon clattered down Front Street. Moses guessed the man driving to be a farmer.

When no others came, Will whispered, "Get ready to run to the building beside the white brick house. All three of us at once."

"Yessir," Moses and Tom answered. Moses clutched Cornpone's rope.

"Now, run!" Will jumped and ran. Behind him the two boys and the dog sprinted, as close as shadows. They ran across the street and through the unlocked door of Mr. Collins' cabinet shop.

"Duck down." Will closed the door.

Moses drew in a deep breath. "Smells like the piney woods behind our cabin."

Tom looked around and pointed. "Those be coffins?"

"Yep. Anyone comes in the next few minutes, that's where we hole up." Will hid a smile. "Not afraid, are you?"

Tom shook his head, but he kept his eye on the coffins.

Will looked around farther and pointed to two old blankets rolled up behind a band saw. "I'd guess those are for you."

Moses pulled them out and revealed several jugs of water and two loaves of bread. "Look here. I be right thirsty."

"And hungry, too." Tom clutched his stomach.

"Take them. You probably have Miz Collins to thank."

The boys finished one loaf, sharing a little with the dog.

"I be tired. Powerful tired." Tom grabbed one of the blankets.

Will led them to the back of the shop, which had piles of lumber, stacked four or five feet high. He pointed to the space between the lumber and the wall. "Crawl back there with your blankets and disappear during the day."

Tom crept in, dragging his blanket. Cornpone crawled in beside him.

Will shook his head. "Not the dog. I'll tie the dog outside. In a few hours, Mr. Collins will be here, working. He knows you're here."

Moses patted Cornpone. "He be good at escapin', so tie him tight."

Will grabbed the rope and pulled the dog to the door. He turned to Moses. "Mr. Collins may have some customers or others come in."

Moses rolled his eyes. "Who?"

"Maybe slave catchers. Maybe a suspicious neighbor." Will pointed to the two windows. "Stay back from the windows. The plan is for you to hide in here all day, then tonight you'll head further north."

Moses looked Will in the eye. "Thanky, sir."

"Call me Will."

"Thanky, Will. I be Moses. The Lord send you to help me and Tom."

"Moses and Tom."

"We be runnin' to Canada."

"Canada's a long way."

"The Lord done deliver us two times already."

Will grasped Moses' arm. "I may never see you again, but I'll pray for your safety."

◄———○———►

Ripley, Ohio

Will slipped out of Mr. Collin's shop and closed the door behind him. As soon as he tied up the dog to the horse rail, he hurried back home. The rain had stopped and the faint glow of dawn showed in the eastern sky. He pulled off his muddy boots outside and sneaked through the back door. *Pa's gun is back in its place.*

In his stocking feet, he tiptoed through the kitchen and up the stairs. *Whew. Nobody woke up. Ah, my own bed sure looks good.*

As soon as his head touched the pillow, he fell into a deep sleep. Even while he slept, his mind replayed scenes from the night before.

"No!" he yelled. Cutter and his gang chased him along the Ohio shore. Will's legs pumped as fast as they could go. One man caught up and grabbed him and shook his arm. Will pushed the hand away, but it held fast.

"Will!" Polly shook her brother's arm. "Wake up. You're having a bad dream."

Will rubbed his eyes and sat up. Bright light streamed in the window and his little brother Jonah stood beside him, staring. He shook his head and looked at Polly. "I…Cutter and his gang…but it was you shaking me, wasn't it?"

"Ma has your breakfast ready and you'll need to leave for work before long."

"Thanks." Will rumpled his little brother's hair. "Run and get my boots for me? They're out by the back door. Bang the mud off them first."

As soon as Jonah was gone, Polly peppered her brother with questions. "Why are your boots outside? And why do they have mud all over them? Did you help those runaways? Is that why you slept in so long? Did you hear anything about the raid on the Rankins?"

"I can't tell you what I was doing. I have to keep it secret." Will groaned a little as he sat up on the edge of the bed. Every muscle in his legs ached. He pulled on clean socks as he heard his brother returning with the boots. "Pa went out last night. He might have gone on the raid, or maybe he helped the Rankins."

Jonah clomped into the room wearing his brother's boots. "I'm big, ain't I? I be big as you someday. Won't I?"

"Maybe even bigger! Thanks for the boots." Will nodded and poked his little brother in the chest.

Polly took Jonah's hand and led him toward the stairs. "Let's let your big brother get dressed. He's in a hurry this morning."

When Will arrived at the table, Pa sipped a cup of coffee. He had dark shadows under his eyes, but he smiled at Will. "Looks like the rain we had overnight is gone. A fine spring morning."

Will nodded and took a big bite of his fried mush. *Pa knows about the rain. Maybe he knows I know, too. Find out everything on our walk to work.*

As the two walked toward the foundry, the sun struggled to chase away the mist swirling above the river. Will pondered just how to start the conversation. He glanced at the dog tied beside the Collins' brick house. *The dog's still there. Hope Mr. Collins gives him a bit to eat. Maybe I'll share my lunch with him on the way home.*

Pa finally broke the silence. "Some in this town figure it's their job to enforce the law."

"The Fugitive Slave Law?"

Pa nodded, staring over the misty river. "Reverend Rankin preaches that God's law is higher."

"And Ma agrees. But I thought ... ." Will stopped. *Pa doesn't know Polly and I heard them talking on the way home from church.*

"You thought I didn't agree."

"Right."

"A man usually doesn't change his mind, I know. That's something we laugh at the ladies for. But God changed my mind when your Ma told me what she'd overheard."

Will turned to face his father.

"Cutter and his evil friends planned a raid last night against the Rankins. I never want to be on the same side as Cutter. Last night I took my gun to stand alongside that brave family."

"Oh, Pa! I hoped you were going to say that."

"As soon as I got inside their house, Brother Rankin barred the door. The older Rankin boys had their rifles, too, and we all watched from the upstairs windows. Didn't have long to wait. The mob, for that's all it was, had been drinking. They hung around and made a lot of loud threats. They had guns, but when they saw our firepower, they left."

"I saw you leave our house."

Pa's jaw dropped as he turned to face Will. "How? Were you out too?"

Will gazed across the Ohio and began his story. He told of glimpsing Cutter start toward the Rankins and the meeting at Three Mile Creek. "I warned Mr. Parker how some men might have planned an ambush for him and the boys. Mr. Parker rowed me and the two runaway boys to a different place. Right now those boys are hiding in Mr. Collins' workshop."

Through the whole tale, Pa kept shaking his head. "You should've told us, you know. But you did right to help those young fugitives."

Will shook his head. "They're maybe twelve, about Polly's age. It's a long way to Canada."

Pa patted Will's shoulder. "They'll make it. Many along the way are ready to help."

Will stopped and looked his father in the eye. "But others will try to put them back into slavery. Pa, I have to know if they make it."

Missing Boys

Ripley, Ohio

Moses and Tom awoke to the sound of hammering. It took several moments for them to remember they were in a cabinet-maker's shop. Light from an unseen window filtered past the stacks of lumber around them. The pounding sounds stopped and sawing began.

"We can set up and have some breakfast," Moses whispered.

Tom nodded and they wriggled out of their blankets. Tom took a swig from the jug and handed it to Moses. They tore hunks of bread from their loaf. They heard whistling along with the pounding.

Moses began to hum along. "Swing low, sweet chariot." He stopped when the door opened and someone came in.

"My wife's cabinet ready?" The man's voice had a nasal sound.

"Sure is. The bill is here somewhere." The boys heard papers being shuffled.

The nasal voice spoke again. "New dog?"

"Yep, a stray. Guess I've got a soft heart."

"You see any fugitives this morning, Collins?"

"Not a single one. Somebody missing his slaves?"

"Two boys missing from the Anderson farm. They was due to get auctioned today at the courthouse."

"Here's the bill. Seven fifty. How'd you find out?"

"Their overseer put up reward papers all around town. Didn't you see them? He looked fit to be tied. Had his whip with him. If he finds them, he'll beat those boys within an inch of their lives."

Moments later the door closed and Mr. Collins went back to whistling.

Tom and Moses shivered.

◄——○——►

John Parker's Foundry, Ripley, Ohio

Will expected the day at the foundry to be a normal workday. He was wrong.

Mr. Parker nodded to Pa and Will as they went to their separate workstations. Will saw Pa and Mr. Parker walk outside and begin to load a wagon.

Will rubbed his chin. *Pa's job has nothing to do with loading wagons. I bet Mr. Parker just wants to talk about something private.*

At lunch, Pa ate quickly and hurried Will along, too. Then he picked up his tin pail and headed home, motioning Will to join him. Will frowned. *We don't go home at lunch. Wonder what's up?*

As soon as they left the foundry, Pa poured out the story of Mr. Parker's escapades. "Last night after he dropped you off in the cove, he rowed his skiff to his own pier and tied it up and went home. He'd no sooner changed to his nightclothes and climbed into bed when he heard an awful pounding on his front door. He leaned out his window and waved his gun at the slave catchers, but they refused to leave till they'd searched his place."

"He probably laughed to himself while they searched," said Will.

"He probably told them where to look. But those bounty hunters aren't going to give up. They're hanging around Ripley for a while." Pa stopped. "But we'd like you to go on a short trip."

"Sure. Where?"

"Collins has two coffins to deliver north of here."

"But, can't he deliver them himself?"

"He could, but he needs your help to deliver something besides the coffins."

"D-dead bodies?"

"No. Live boys."

"Moses and Tom." Will laughed. "When do I leave?"

"Mid-afternoon. I'll have Ma pack you and the boys a cold supper and I'll deliver it to Mr. Collins. You go on back to work at the foundry till then."

Thomas Collins' Cabinet Shop, Ripley, Ohio

Moses and Tom finished all of their bread and water. Their bodies begged to unbend from the cramped hiding place, but they knew they had to stay quiet.

Mr. Collins sawed, whistling as he worked. The noise stopped and new noises began, so Moses strained to listen. *Sounds like a bolt bein' slid. Now, a rollin' door. Jingle of harness. A horse nicker. The cabinet man be goin' somewhere. Maybe we be goin', too.*

Another person came into the shop. Tom got excited. "Sound like—that boy what help us. Will be his name."

Moses shushed Tom so he could listen better.

"I like your new dog, Mr. Collins."

Mr. Collins' laugh rumbled like far-off thunder. "I guessed that mutt had some connection to our special cargo."

Moses smiled at Tom. "We be special."

Moses heard Mr. Collins giving Will directions. "Your ma brought these over about an hour ago. Put them on the springboard seat and help me load the wagon."

"Yes, sir."

"This coffin's going. Help me set one end on this dolly. We can move it easy."

"I've got this end. This is heavy. Good thing it's empty."

"Most of the ones I deliver aren't full yet. The coffins are for a man and his wife who're still alive and kicking. They want to be ready when the Lord calls them home, so ordered their coffins ahead."

"I suppose everybody should be ready," Will said.

"That smaller coffin's going, too. We can load it the same way."

Mr. Collins' voice came from far away, mixed with grunting and bumping. "That does it. Now to load our other cargo."

Will said, "I wouldn't like to travel in there. At least it has a few air holes."

"Tell the boys to grab their blankets and their jug and slide in here as fast and quiet as they can."

Moses climbed out. "We be ready."

Tom emerged next and saw the coffins. He grabbed Moses' arm and turned to run. "No, sir. No sir. This boy ain't ridin' in no coffin."

Will shook his head. "Right. Not a coffin, a secret compartment." He pointed to an opening in the floor below the coffins. "Here's your vittles. My ma packed one for me, too."

Moses and Tom climbed inside and hunkered down and Mr. Collins slid the panel closed.

Tom clutched Moses' arm. "I hate bein' in small spaces."

Moses patted his hand. "We be safe here."

"We taking their dog, Mr. Collins?" Will asked.

Moses held his breath. The answer was hard to hear, but he thought it was yes.

"Where'd you get this wagon with a secret compartment?" asked Will.

"Had it built special. Climb aboard. We got miles to go."

In their narrow space, Moses and Tom felt each bump of the rutted road. Moses peeked through an air hole and breathed in. "Smell like springtime. Look like freedom."

"This don't feel like no chariot," said Tom.

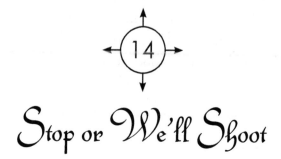

Stop or We'll Shoot

On the way to the Gist Settlement

Will enjoyed riding with Mr. Collins, because of his stories about the Underground Railroad. Cornpone sat at Will's feet.

"We won't wait till tonight to do a transfer," Mr. Collins said. "Parker thinks those slave catchers will make trouble. Their interest in the Fugitive Slave Law is the reward money."

"Do the slave catchers know about you?"

"They've nearly caught me with fugitives in my workshop."

"Are you worried about fines or jail time?'

"Of course, but there's a higher law."

"You mean the Bible?"

"The Bible may not say much about slavery, but it tells us how to treat other people. Do unto others as you would have them do unto you."

"I'd hate to be a slave, or get whipped or taken away from my family," Will said.

The wagon jolted across a rut and they heard someone cry "Ow!"

"Those boys feel every bump," Mr. Collins said. "But they can stretch their legs in less than an hour."

"Where we going?"

"Ever hear of the Gist Settlement?"

"Nope."

"A man named Gist wrote in his will that his slaves would be set free and given land. About a hundred and fifty of them got land in Ohio. Their settlement is struggling though. It's poor land for farming."

"Close to Ripley?"

"Yep. You take the boys there. I'm going farther to deliver these coffins." Mr. Collins' voice dropped. "I never write down directions. Here's the way, so listen. Up ahead is a—"

They heard horses galloping up behind them.

"Somebody's in a hurry," Mr. Collins said.

"Is it slave catchers?" Will's stomach rose to his throat.

Two men on horseback galloped up a minute later and reined their mounts to match the speed of the wagon. Will's heart pounded. Cornpone, sitting at Will's feet, gave a low growl and bared his teeth. Will grabbed the dog's rope.

"Whoa!" The man in front leaned toward them and waved his pistol. "Collins, stop your wagon or we'll shoot."

Mr. Collins pulled on the reins. He answered the men as if he were passing the time of day. "Put that away, Knight. I'm in no hurry to fill up one of my coffins."

"Keep that dog under control. I may need to use my gun after all."

Will's teeth began to chatter, so he clamped his mouth closed. He looked away from the gun and stared at Knight's black horse. A white star blazed on its forehead.

"Hughes, check inside them pine boxes to make sure they're empty." Knight motioned to his fellow rider, a skinny man with stringy blond hair, to climb up into the wagon.

"Go right ahead." Mr. Collins shrugged.

The man tried to lift the lid of the larger coffin, but it stuck. He demanded a tool from Mr. Collins.

He shook his head. "Left my tools back in the shop."

Knight leaned forward and scowled. "Unless we can check these two boxes, you two ain't going nowhere."

Will slid his hand into his pocket and whispered, "Shall I offer my knife?" When Mr. Collins nodded, Will held it out.

Knight grabbed the knife without a word and handed it to his accomplice. Hughes forced the lid and looked inside. "Empty. I'll check the other." He opened the second one without the help of the knife, but instead of returning it to Will, he slipped it into his pocket.

"Can I have my knife back, sir?"

Knight sneered. "That's a pretty fancy knife for a young kid like you. Probably stole it."

"No, I didn't steal it," said Will.

Hughes' mocking laugh cut the air. "Well, I did." He climbed back on his horse. "Don't figure on ever seein' it again."

The two men rode on ahead, pushing their horses to a gallop.

Mr. Collins slapped the reins on his horses' backs. "Giddap." He turned to Will. "Those men live outside the law now, but someday they'll meet a lawless end."

Will was shaking, from both anger and fear. "They coming back?"

"Maybe. If it's after you and the boys are gone, they'll be suspicious," Mr. Collins said.

"What would they do?"

"They'd start hunting for you, combing the area between here and there. The big reward they earn makes all their effort worthwhile. Make sure they don't find you."

Will gripped the dog's rope collar. "Tell me how to get there."

"We're coming to a crossroads in about five miles. I'm going straight, but I'll stop a ways beyond it and let you and the boys out. You're to follow the crossroad to the right, but stay out of sight."

"The road leads to the Gist Settlement?"

"Not directly. In less than two miles it forks to the left. Go one more mile on the left fork, and cross the stream ahead of you."

"Is it deep?"

"No, you can ford it on the rocks, just watch not to slip on them. After the stream, climb the hill and follow the trail for four miles or so. At the first cabin, ask for anyone in the Johnson family."

Will repeated the directions back to Mr. Collins to make sure he could remember them. "But how will I get back home?"

"Meet me at the crossroads tomorrow noon. I'll be on my way back from delivering these coffins."

They rode on in silence, watching the road ahead for the two horsemen to return. At every sound from the deep woods, Will jumped. *Wonder if there's a wildcat in there?*

Mr. Collins pointed ahead. "There's the crossroads. We'll take the chance Knight and Hughes have gone elsewhere."

As soon as the wagon stopped, Will and Cornpone hopped down. Mr. Collins slid the panel open and the boys scrambled out and stretched their legs.

Moses nodded to Mr. Collins. "Sir, I be mighty grateful for your kindness."

"We need to hurry." Will chewed his lower lip. "It'll start getting dark in another hour."

The cabinetmaker climbed back into the seat and clucked to the horses. "The Lord be with you, boys."

Trying to put on a brave face, Will waved goodbye and turned to Moses and Tom. "Let's get out of sight."

Three boys and one dog melted into the woods.

Through the Woods

North of Ripley, Ohio

Will stopped when they were out of sight of the road. "We might get separated." He pulled Tom and Moses close. They stood in a circle and he outlined the directions. Cornpone stuck his nose in, like he wanted to listen, too.

"Where we goin'?" Tom asked.

"It's called the Gist Settlement. All that live there are free Negroes."

Moses stared with his mouth open. "Free? And have they own land? And nobody to whip 'em?" He shook his head as if this was beyond belief.

"I've never been there, but that's what Mr. Collins says. Those slave catchers who stopped us on the road might be looking for us, though."

Moses touched his fingers as he repeated each step of the route. He reached down to pat Cornpone. "Lord, keep us on the way."

Will shuddered with fear. The three passed through the trackless woods by keeping the road in sight. Cornpone trailed them, his nose to the ground.

They followed the leftward fork in the road, really just two wagon tracks, till it ended in the stream. The water sparkled with the late afternoon sun and they all stopped for a drink. Stepping from rock to rock, they had just reached the far side when they heard horses.

Will scanned the stream bank for the best place to hide. The woods by the stream had thinned, so he pointed downstream. "Follow me into the brush beside the bank there." He sprinted, tailed by Moses, Tom and Cornpone. They reached the thicket moments before the two horsemen came to the edge of the stream.

Will peeked through the brush and caught sight of the men. *The slave catchers! They'll see our footprints, for sure.*

The horses leaned down to drink. Knight studied the ground beside the stream. "We're on their trail now!"

"But which way did they go?" Hughes took off his hat and wiped his brow. He leaned forward in the saddle and looked downstream.

Will hissed, "Don't move a muscle! If they come this direction, run."

Moses closed his eyes and murmured a prayer. "Lord, keep us safe from them slave catchers."

The man on the black horse pointed downstream. Will groaned. "They're coming this way. Crawl on your bellies back toward the woods. Stay out of sight until they're right across from us."

The horsemen made plenty of noise, splashing through the water. Will couldn't hear what they said, but he hoped they hadn't seen them.

When the boys were halfway up the hill to the woods, the two men gave a shout. Will stood to run and called to Moses and Tom to follow. They raced to the trees, crashing through the underbrush.

As he slowed to see how the other two were doing, Will nearly tripped.

Moses, with Cornpone at his side, called to Tom, still ten steps back. "Faster, faster, or they gonna get you." Beyond Tom he could see the men at the edge of the woods. They dismounted and tied their horses and plunged into the woods after the boys.

The boys kept running and reached the top of the hill. Ahead they could see a trail that led beside a deep ravine.

Will looked at the men and judged they were a good way off. "Let's run to that ravine and see if we can find a good hiding place."

Moses and Tom nodded and took off running beside Will. The crest of the hill hid them as they slid down the bank of the ravine. A stream bubbled at the bottom, but Will avoided it, fearing they'd leave footprints. The three boys fanned out in all directions, desperate for a hiding place.

Moses ran ahead and investigated a huge fallen tree beyond the stream. The beech tree had given up its struggle to stay upright after the spring rains had washed away the soil from its roots. The area under the trunk had soil piled up on one side, forming a natural cave.

Moses waved to Will, careful not to shout. He pointed to the narrow opening and Will nodded. Tom and Cornpone joined them, slid under the tree, and disappeared. Once inside, Will used a branch to eliminate the footprints they'd left. They walled off the entrance from the inside with sticks and leaves, making their hiding place almost invisible.

The boys held their breath and listened to the noise of branches breaking in the distance. The slave catchers called to each other as they hunted for their quarry. The boys heard their heavy breathing when they stopped close to their hiding place.

"How in tarnation did those three boys disappear? And that mangy dog?" Knight asked.

Hughes' voice rose in anger. "I swear they must have split up and run in three different directions."

Knight snarled an idea that made the boys shudder. "Sic some hounds on 'em. Track 'em in no time at all."

"We don't have time for that. Some foul fellow might be stealing our horses right now."

"I'd hate to walk all the way back to Ripley."

"Before we give up, let's walk farther down the trail."

"I thought I heard them in this ravine when we first crested the hill."

"They ain't up a tree. The spring leaves are too small to hide them."

The men's voices faded as they walked back up the side of the ravine to the trail. Soon the boys heard only birds chirping and a nearby squirrel scolding.

Will let out a big breath. "That was close."

Moses breathed a prayer. "Thanky, Lord."

"I be stayin' here for a spell." Tom held tight to Cornpone.

"Me, too," Moses said.

"What made you both run from Kentucky? It might cost your life."

"The overseer say I be no account and lazy," said Tom. "Master Simon goin' to sell me down river. That be the death of me."

"Cyrus, he the overseer. Last week he done whip me. He say I be workin' too slow." Moses pulled his shirt up to show the scabs from the whipping.

Will's stomach tightened in sympathy.

"My mammy got whipped to death for learnin' me my letters," Moses said.

Will caught his breath. "That's right. It's against the law to teach a slave to read."

"When I be free, I learn to read," Moses said.

"Here's a word you can learn today." Will picked up a stick and scratched letters in the soft dirt. "F R E E D O M."

Moses tilted his head and whispered the letters. "F-R-E-E-D-O-M. What be the word?"

"Freedom."

Moses repeated the word as if it were something holy. "Freedom. Now I can read somethin'."

"Remember that paper on the tree?" Tom asked. "Mr. Parker told us it say they give thousand dollar for Mr. Parker, dead or alive."

"A thousand dollars? He said there'd be a reward for you two. He guessed two hundred each," said Will.

"We ain't worth near as much as Mr. Parker," said Moses.

Tom snickered. "But only if we be alive."

"Since I'm the least valuable, I'll go scout out to see if those slave catchers have quit looking for us," said Will. "I'll circle way around the other side of this ravine and check to make sure their horses are gone from the edge of the woods."

Will slipped out and worked his way toward the stream, away from the trail. It took much longer than their headlong run into the woods, and Will worried about the lengthening shadows.

Three Against Two

Ripley, Ohio

Soon after Will left, Moses and Tom heard the slave catchers talking in the distance. They froze in fear. Twigs snapped as the men got closer. It was too late to rebuild the stick-and-leaf wall that had hidden them.

Moses heart stopped when Hughes spoke just outside their hiding place. "No sign of them farther on."

"This fallen tree looks mighty suspicious." Knight leaned down and poked a stick in the hole. Tom shrank back, but the stick stabbed his arm. "Hughes, someone's in there!"

"Sure it's them runaways and not a possum?"

Cornpone began to growl. He lunged out the opening toward the two men, snarling.

Knight attacked the dog with his stick. Cornpone bared his teeth and raced toward Knight's legs.

"That dog was with Collins and that boy." Hughes grabbed a sharp stick and slashed at the dog's back. Cornpone yelped and blood dripped from a gash. "Come out, all of you, or I'll kill the dog."

Moses looked at Tom and shook his head. They didn't move.

Cornpone barked and Hughes hit him again with his stick. Knight grabbed the trailing rope and tied him to a nearby tree.

Knight hurled a taunt into the hiding place. "We'll start a fire and burn you out."

Tom's eyes opened wide and he whispered, "Anythin' but burnin'. Too much like hell. I be goin' out."

"Hold off. We be comin' out," Moses said.

As soon as Tom wriggled out, Knight smirked and grabbed his wrists. Hughes tied his arms behind his back, leaving a leash. Moments later, Moses got the same treatment.

"Where's that boy who was with you?" Knight yanked on Moses' rope.

Moses shook his head.

"Check inside that cave," Knight said.

Hughes ducked down and peered inside. "He ain't there."

"Let's get out of here before that young buck comes to make trouble." He shoved Moses and Tom ahead. "Run out just as fast as you ran in here."

When the slave catchers reached their horses, Knight found some more rope. He waved it at Hughes. "Tie up their feet so they can't run off."

The men slung the roped bundles behind their saddles, like lumpy bedrolls. They rode down the hill, through the stream, and back toward Ripley in the gathering twilight.

Moses squeezed his eyes shut and prayed hard. *Lord, help us. Or we never get loose from all this rope.*

Will looked everywhere around the beech tree. He was sick when he realized the boys were gone. *How could they snatch them away from here so fast?*

Cornpone whimpered and nuzzled Will's hand as he untied him. "We'll find them. They can't be far ahead."

He raced up the ravine, the dog at his heels, back along the trail, and down the hill. He raced through the stream following the hoof prints of the horses. Panting, he leaned against a tree to catch his breath. By the time he reached the wagon tracks of the fork in the road, his side ached and his lungs felt ready to burst. *Lord, help me find them. Probably headed back to Ripley. How can I rescue them?*

Glancing at the dark woods on either side of the road, Will ran a little faster, glad to have the dog at his side. *Sure hope someone will come along and give me a ride. Too far to run all the way.*

His chest felt like it had an iron strap around it, but he knew he had to keep running. *Tired. Those boys back in chains. Oh, Lord, no.*

Hearing hoof beats behind him, he jogged to the side of the road. The horse, dapple-gray, had seen hard work that day, judging by its caked-on dirt. The rider was a short older man dressed in work clothes. Will waved at him and he stopped.

"What's the matter, young feller?"

Will paused to catch his breath. *Can't tell the whole story, but I'm no good at telling lies.* "Um, I was doing an errand for my pa, and it took longer, and now I'm late getting back home to Ripley."

The man leaned over and offered Will his strong arm. "You're welcome to hitch a ride behind me on Jenny. My name's Reynolds, David Reynolds."

Will smiled his thanks, put his foot in the stirrup and mounted behind the man. "Name's Will Butler. Been running for miles. Thanks for the ride."

"Yep, it'll be dark before too long."

"These woods safe?"

The man laughed. "Worried about wild animals or dangerous people?"

"Either one." Will swallowed, wondering what the man would say next.

"Depends on what color you are. If you was black, you'd be in danger from bounty hunters, southern sympathizers, and people like me who just want this country to ourselves."

Will changed the subject to something safe. "How far is it to Ripley from here?"

"Oh, I'd guess we got another hour, maybe."

Will tried to talk for a while, but was so tired he couldn't think straight. He closed his eyes, relaxed by the steady clip-clop of the horse. His head fell forward against the man's back and he dozed.

Dinner for Two

Ripley, Ohio

Knight and Hughes drew close to Ripley with their captured runaways. Dusk brought shadows to the woods around them.

Moses fought a feeling of despair. *This be the same way we come with Will. Tom and me be headed back to Kentucky.*

"Pretty good day's work, don't you think?" Knight asked his friend.

"The posters for these two, what was the reward?"

"Two hundred each. The price is high since they're young and strong," Knight said.

"Calls for a celebration. I'm ready for a good supper at Mrs. Bennington's."

"Makes me hungry just thinking about her pork chops. Are you buying?" Knight urged his horse to a canter.

"You're the rich one." Hughes laughed. "We gonna feed the runaways?"

"They should've stayed home if they wanted regular meals," Knight said.

When the men arrived at Mrs. Bennington's, eight other horses swished their tails by the hitching post. The slave catchers left the boys tied on their horses, and joined the regular customers at one of the wooden tables in the narrow room.

Moses called to Tom, "Leastways they didn't whip us."

"Cyrus will. He be in a fury."

"This still be free land."

"We ain't free, nohow," said Tom.

Moses closed his eyes. *Lord, you still there? Lord, we sure need your help.*

←——○——→

"Sonny, we're getting close to Ripley." Mr. Reynolds nudged Will awake.

Will opened his eyes and shook his head a little. "Sorry, sir. I didn't mean to go to sleep."

"Jenny's got a nice even gait. We've gone many miles together. I've napped a few times on her back, myself."

Will recognized the northern edge of Ripley when they passed a white frame house in need of paint. One sniff reminded him they were close to the tannery. He craned his neck to see if the dog had kept pace. Cornpone, nose to the ground, trotted a few paces back.

Mr. Reynolds pulled his horse up at a frame house with a new coat of red paint and a small red barn behind it. "That's my house and barn."

Will slid off the back of the horse. "Mr. Reynolds, much obliged for the ride and the nap. I'll walk on down to Front Street. That's where I live."

Will hurried toward the river, trying to decide what to do next. He stopped short, staring. There, tied up at Mrs. Bennington's, he saw a familiar black horse with a white star. *The slave catchers. Those strange bedrolls behind the saddles, why, that's Moses and Tom!*

Will ran up to Moses, tied on Knight's horse. "I'm so glad I found you before they took you across the river."

"The knife, my pocket," Moses said.

Will began to cut the rope from Moses' hands. "You next, Tom."

Will heard voices at the door and slid the knife back into Moses' pocket. He ducked behind the black horse.

Knight stood in the doorway and yelled back at his friend. "Get that bottle from the table."

Will slipped behind the other horses tied to the rail just as the men came to the hitching post.

Hughes mounted his horse and slid the bottle into his saddlebag. "How long will we be waiting to cross the river? Maybe we'll need another bottle."

"I've got one in my saddlebag. Let's get going." Knight laughed and swung his leg over his saddle without even glancing at Moses.

Will crept away into the dark shadows. *Got to get them free before they cross the river.*

He watched the horses disappear in the fading light and ran to follow them.

Front Street, Ripley, Ohio

Knight and Hughes rode along Front Street, nearly deserted at that time of evening. Their horses picked their way down a rocky trail to the river's edge. Several skiffs bobbed in the water, but no one else was in sight. They tied their horses to a tree and rolled the fugitives off.

Tom cried out in pain, but Knight just laughed. "You'll holler louder when your overseer gets a turn with his whip."

Hughes dug into his saddlebag for the half-empty bottle. "How soon before your buddy comes?"

Knight made himself comfortable on a fallen log. "He'll be here when he gets here." He opened the new bottle he'd brought and took a swig.

Moses wriggled to a more comfortable position and tested the ropes around his wrists. *Will cut the knots some. Just keep workin'. Get free. Help Tom.*

The men were getting louder as they talked about what they'd do with all the money they'd get for the runaways.

Moses got his hands free, but left the ropes on his wrists, in case the men looked his way. *We be in the shadows. Get my legs free. Move close to Tom.* He used the knife to cut the knot holding his legs and crept toward Tom.

"They goin' to grab us if you don't hurry," said Tom.

"They be drinkin'. They cain't run so fast. Just wait," said Moses.

Tom nodded and looked around to spy out a good escape route. His eyes widened when he saw a shadowy figure slithering down the hill toward them. Tom pointed and hissed, "It be Will! And our dog with him."

Moses grinned and held his hands apart to show Will the ropes no longer bound them.

Through hand signals, Will told them to wait. He crept beyond them past the horses and hunted some large stones. Hidden, he howled like a coyote and threw stones toward the horses. They bucked, yanked their reins loose and cantered along the shore. Will scrambled up the hill, hoping he wouldn't be spotted.

"What's going on?" Hughes shouted. The slave catchers jumped to their feet and ran to catch the horses.

Moses hissed at Tom. "Now's our chance!" They clambered up the rocky hill toward Front Street and found Cornpone waiting for them.

Knight chased the black horse, calling, "Whoa, Blaze."

Hughes caught his horse first and galloped to catch Blaze.

"Get him! He spooked the horses," Knight yelled, pointing at Will.

Will reached Front Street at the same time Moses and Tom did. He raced toward his own house, waving to them to follow. He saw a few people on the street, but no one he knew. Just after they slipped onto a side street, he heard heavy footsteps behind them on Front Street.

"Stop those boys!" Knight shouted.

Will led them down the alley behind his house. "There's our garden shed. Hide there." He opened the door and the fugitives ducked into the shed, with Cornpone at their heels. "I'll be back later."

Will latched the shed door and raced into the house. The kitchen was empty. "Ma, Pa, anybody home?"

Jonah ran to hug him. "Ma said you were gone till tomorrow."

Polly peeked around the corner. "You're too late for dinner. You're not supposed to be home yet."

Ma bustled in with a worried look on her face. "You're panting. Did something go wrong?"

Will nodded. "Where's Pa?"

She pointed to the family parlor. "Shall I fix you something to eat?"

Will nodded. "Fix three dinners."

Polly rolled her eyes. "You can't eat that much!"

Pa's tall figure filled the doorway. "He's a growing boy. But why are you here, son?"

Ma raised her hand. "Tell us in a minute. Let me put the young-uns to bed first." She lowered her voice. "Little pitchers have big ears."

When Ma returned, she and Pa and Polly surrounded Will as he perched on a stool and spilled out a short version of his adventures.

"The boys and their dog are hiding in our garden shed. The slave catchers even chased us down Front Street, but we lost them in the alley behind our house."

Pa's face turned white. "So you're marked as one who aided fugitives?"

"I don't think they saw my face tonight. But, I was marked when they saw me with Mr. Collins." Will rubbed his chin. "How can I get word to Mr. Collins I won't be at the crossroads?"

Ma heaped applesauce beside the thick slices of ham and cornbread on all three plates. "Henry, shall I have Polly take the food out?"

Pa's brow furrowed as he considered his answer. "No. Let Will do it. Then we can stand before the judge and truthfully say we haven't seen any fugitives."

Ma looked him in the eye. "I'd much rather have a clear conscience when I stand before God at Judgment Day."

Pa was silent a long time. "You preach a powerful sermon." He sighed and shook his head. "I keep getting in deeper and deeper. I'm hatching a plan. Hannah, do you have an extra gown? I'll need one from you, too, Polly. And two bonnets."

Will raised his eyebrows. "That's a bold idea, if it's what I think."

Pa nodded. "Let's pray right now for the Lord's help with the whole thing. Then I'll head over to ask Parker if he needs a delivery made up north. If he does, I'll put a note for Mr. Collins at the crossroads."

Two Girls of Ripley

Ripley, Ohio

As soon as Will closed the door, Moses and Tom fumbled their way into the back corner of the garden shed, bumping into boxes and tools on their way.

"Oww!" Tom's shin cracked against something in the dark.

Moses hissed, "Sssh! Just set where you be."

Both boys stroked Cornpone to calm their pounding hearts. They hunched in their dark hideout, listening for the heavy tread of slave catchers.

"Moses?" Tom's voice trembled. "Is you sorry you run off with me?"

"Nope. I be glad."

"Be it a far piece to Canada?"

"Too far to think on. Think on the way the Lord done rescued us two times already."

"When I be free, I goin' to be rich."

"Rich people get lots of troubles from what I see," Moses said.

"When I be free, I be my own boss and have my own house."

"When I be free, I learn to read. I can go help your folks and Grampa and our brothers and sisters."

"If Cyrus see me ever again, he whip me dead."

Moses put his hand on Tom's shoulder. "No more whippin' in freedom land."

"I hate that devil."

"Forget Cyrus."

"Cyrus sure to whip Mammy and Pappy next." Tom sighed. "I miss them."

Moses tensed as he heard footsteps. "Ssh!"

The door opened and they recognized Will's shape in the doorway. He closed the door and spoke just above a whisper. "Tom? Moses? I brought you something to eat."

"We be in this corner," Tom said. Will stepped closer and gave them the plates of food. He bent down and gave the dog two squares of cornbread.

Moses took a bite of ham. "That slave catcher, he find you?"

"Not yet. But he knows about Mr. Collins. He may track you here." Will handed them a jug of water to share. "We're going to try a different route to Canada."

"We be ready. Tonight?"

"First thing in the morning." Will slid the handle of a cloth bag from his shoulder. "Put these dresses on right over your clothes. The yellow dress is bigger, so it's for Tom."

"We ain't had no practice bein' girls." Tom reached for the bag.

"Well, girls are a different shape. You know, up front. So there's extra rags to stuff in that part of the dresses."

"Bonnets, too?" Moses asked.

"Yep, they're in the bag. Wish we had wigs for you. My pa is making a delivery in the wagon. His two brand new daughters are going along for the ride."

"But when they see we ain't the right color, they grab us," Tom said.

Will tried to reassure him. "Just keep your heads down. And hide your hands under your skirt. Leaving early means not many folks will be about. Especially those two who chased us."

"They was gettin' whiskeyed," Moses said.

"They'll probably have a big headache tomorrow." Will felt his way to the door. "Tom and Moses, I may never see you again. I-I wanted to tell you how brave I think you are."

Moses touched Will's arm. "The Lord, He send you at the right time."

Tom set the jug down and reached to shake Will's hand. "Mose and me, this time we agree."

Ripley to Red Oak

Dawn streaked the sky with orange and pink as Pa pulled his wagon to a stop in the alley behind the Butler house. Tools from the foundry, packed in straw, filled the back of the wagon. Pa helped two bonneted figures to the springboard seat and climbed up between them. On his left perched a figure in a yellow dress. On the other side, a slightly smaller figure sat, adjusting a bonnet. A yellow dog with one bent ear sat by the wagon, as if hoping for a ride.

"Young ladies keep their knees together, even under their dresses." Pa elbowed Moses, who sat with hands on his spread-apart knees.

Moses pulled the skirt straight. "Yessir, Mr. Butler."

Tom's dress had wrapped around his feet. "This dress be too long. Hope I don't have to run."

Most of the households in Ripley had started to stir as the wagon jolted past. A woman emptied a basin out her side door and stared at them.

"Keep your heads down. There are plenty in this town who'd turn you in for the reward, without batting an eye. And that woman is one of them."

A few roosters crowed at them and a pair of dogs ran up to Cornpone. Tom quivered. "Them hounds, I don't like 'em."

Moses smiled. "They just bein' friendly."

Pa pointed to a sheet of white paper on a tree beside the road. "That handbill worries me. Probably has your descriptions and a reward."

Moses saw handbills on every tree. "This freedom be dangerous." Each paper had the silhouettes of two fleeing slaves.

"How far we be goin' today?" Tom asked.

Pa slapped the reins on the horses' backs. "Our goal is a church in Red Oak, about two hours from here."

The early-morning birds chirped as the wagon rolled along the rutted road. An army of robins hopped along, hunting for worms in the newly-plowed and planted fields.

Moses remembered the furrows he'd plowed just a few days ago. *Them robins find the worms. Hope them slave catchers cain't find Tom and me.*

When the fields gave way to woods, the three in the wagon relaxed a little. The spring sunshine felt good after the early morning coolness. Cornpone took a few side trips, investigating noises and smells.

Moses began to hum his favorite tune, Swing Low, Sweet Chariot. "Our Grampa be the song leader on the Lord's Day. We have singin' and preachin'."

"Singin' help us through our trials," Tom said.

Pa glanced around to see that no one was nearby. "Those trials are for our good, I've learned."

"I don't like 'em at all," said Tom.

Pa told them about the raid on the Rankin house. "That trial made me choose which side I ought to be fighting for."

Near Red Oak, Pa noticed a figure on the road ahead. "That man's probably a local farmer or a laborer of some sort. I'll not offer him a ride, though, so keep your heads turned as we pass him."

As they got closer, Tom said, "Why, he be a black man." He wore a red plaid shirt and a straw hat and whistled a tune as he strode along.

Pa nodded to the man as the wagon passed. "Nice day." The man nodded and tipped his hat.

When they'd gone beyond the hiker, Pa shook his head. "He's probably a free black. Even so, he's not safe walking along in broad daylight by himself. Slave catchers aren't too careful who they snatch, sometimes."

Moses yanked at the skirt. "Seems like ain't no place safe, 'cept Canada."

"Look on all the trees. More handbills about you boys." Pa glanced behind him. "That man had one hanging out his back pocket."

"But he be black," Tom said.

Pa shook his head. "Some think money's worth more than a clear conscience."

Their wagon rattled into the village of Red Oak. Moses tensed when a few citizens turned to watch the strangers. The livery stable reeked of the smell of horse manure. They passed the blacksmith's forge and heard the clang of hammer against iron.

At the far end of town, Pa pulled the wagon to a stop in front of a stone church building. Beyond it, a white frame house stood at the end of a row of trees.

Pa helped the boys, awkward in their dresses, to the ground. "Try to behave like young ladies. Lift the front of the skirts so you can walk better."

The boys tried to follow directions. Tom lifted his skirt so high that his pants showed. Moses hurried so much he stumbled and fell down. Cornpone, dusty and tired, kept close to the boys.

Pa glanced around to see if anyone watched the parade. He stepped to the door of the house and knocked three times.

A plump woman opened the door. "Come in, come in," she said, as she stretched out her hand. "Yes, even the dog. We didn't expect company, but we're always glad to see visitors." Gray curls peeked out from her cap and she had smile lines around her eyes and mouth.

Pa stepped inside after the boys and closed the door. "My name's Henry Butler, from Ripley. I can't stay. I just wanted to make sure these boys were welcome."

"Let me call the Reverend." She rang a hand bell on a table. "Boys, you say?" The lady lifted the edge of Tom's bonnet.

Pa grinned and pointed first to one and then the other. "This is Moses and this is Tom."

"Oh, yes, the Reverend showed me a handbill he found in town this morning. Yes, we can find a spot for them both."

A white-haired man with bushy black eyebrows filled the doorway behind her. "We certainly can. Thanks for bringing them."

Pa stepped forward to shake his hand. "Thanks, Reverend. Henry Butler here. I've come to town to deliver tools for the Parker foundry. Can you take the boys farther north?"

The Reverend drew his thick brows together. "The dog, too?"

Moses and Tom looked worried until they saw the Reverend grin and lean down to pat Cornpone. "We've got just enough space for one dog and two boys."

Pa put his hat back on. "The sooner I get back to Ripley, the less suspicion I'll arouse."

"Red Oak, same as Ripley, buzzes with suspicions," the Reverend said.

Pa turned to the boys. "These fine people will take good care of you. Do exactly what they say."

"Yessir," Moses and Tom said.

"Can we take off these bonnets?" Tom asked.

"And these dresses?" Moses pulled on the skirt.

"That's up to the Reverend. Might need them for the next leg of your journey." Pa turned to go. "The Lord keep you safe on your way to Canada."

Moses peeked out the front window to watch Pa leave. "There be that black man in the straw hat." Moses jumped back out of sight. "We seen him walkin' on the road to town."

The Reverend watched the man and frowned. As soon as the Butler wagon disappeared, the man turned toward the house. "Quick, let's get you down cellar. We've got a secret hiding place you'll be safe."

Tom and Moses hustled after the big man, with Cornpone close behind. The preacher called last minute directions to his wife. "That fellow's name is Jack Bailey. Keep watching him. He may come to the door. I think he's an informant. I'll settle the boys and their dog, then slip out to the barn."

In the cellar, the Reverend showed the boys a gap at the base of shelves loaded with jars of pickles, cherries, and applesauce.

"Crawl through, then slide the door closed and bolt it. I'll stack up jars in front."

As soon as they bolted the door, they heard the clunk of jars and then the scrape of a door closing.

"The Reverend, he puts me in mind of Grampa," Tom whispered.

"S'pose he can sing good as Grampa?" Moses looked around with a smile. "This room be all fixed for runaways." Slits of light from narrow openings above the shelves revealed sleeping mats and blankets. A table in the corner held a candle, a basket of crackers, and a jug of water. Cornpone curled up under the table beside the slop jar.

The boys waited long minutes in silence. Moses struggled out of his gown and hung it on a peg.

"Confound dress!" Tom wrestled with the sleeves of the unfamiliar clothing.

Moses pulled the gown over his cousin's head, grinning. "You be such a pretty girl, Tom."

Tom sat on a bench and crossed his arms. "How many days we been runnin'?"

"Three?" Moses shook his head.

"Seem like three years." Cornpone put his head in Tom's lap, as if in sympathy.

Moses grabbed a book from a shelf and showed it to Tom. "This book be for us to read."

"You cain't read, remember?" Tom laughed.

Moses opened the book and pointed to an A and the word beside it. "This be a A, and this say apple, see?"

Tom leaned toward the book and pointed. "What be that letter?"

"That one be a B, and this say baby." Moses kept on through the whole book, calling out the letters he'd learned from his mother and guessing the words from the pictures.

Tom gave his cousin an admiring look. "Teach me letters, too."

"Sure. Let's start now. You cain't get rich 'less you can read." Moses closed his eyes. *Thank the Lord, I be rich already. I be free!*

Bounty Hunters

Ripley, Ohio

Pa finished supper and pushed back from the table. "I suppose you want to hear all about my trip to Red Oak?"

Will had asked Pa lots of questions at work and on the walk home, without success. Pa said he wanted to tell the story only once. Will waited even longer, till Polly and Ma had cleared the table and put away the food.

Meanwhile, Will took the three younger children to the family parlor. Soon Jonah was busy directing Hope and Charity how to march their Noah's Ark animals two by two across the floor. They didn't even notice when he slipped away.

Pa leaned back in his chair. "The trip went smoothly and the boys played their parts well. The old Reverend and his wife up there will take good care of those two. But … ." Pa shifted in his chair. "That gossipy woman on Main Street, Mrs. Williams, stared at us as we left town. She probably guessed that my two passengers were not my wife and daughter."

Ma glanced at Polly. "What will she do?"

Will tapped the table. "Mr. Parker says the slave catchers are still in town. He heard about them chasing us up Main Street."

"If they'd caught you … ." Ma frowned. "I'm frightened to think what would have happened."

Pa leaned forward and gripped the table. "Parker says they swear they'll get those boys yet. So they're asking around town. If Mrs. Williams mentions her suspicions to anyone with a connection to those two bounty hunters, they can easily follow their trail."

"But how will they know where you took the boys?" Ma asked.

"Several in Red Oak noticed us. We saw a free black walking near the village. Even a free black would be in danger from slave catchers unless … ." Pa stopped and drew his brows together in a scowl.

"Unless what, Pa?" Polly chewed her lower lip.

"Unless the black man was a spy?" Will guessed that's what his pa meant.

Pa nodded. "A spy or an informant."

"So that man saw you take them to the safe house?" Ma asked.

"He sure did. When I climbed into the wagon after I delivered the boys, he was a block away." Pa covered his face with his hands. "I've put those boys in danger because I delivered them in daylight."

Ma stood and put her arm on her husband's shoulder. "Don't forget, even in danger, they're in the Lord's hand."

Red Oak, Ohio

After dark, the lady of the house called to the boys in the hidden room. "You can come on out, now. We've got the shades closed. You and the dog can join us in the kitchen for supper."

She moved the jars and they crawled out, grinning. "Supper sounds fine to me, Ma'am," Tom said.

"You can call me Granny Annie." She led them up the stairs into a warm kitchen lit by candles.

Moses smelled fresh bread and the stew bubbling on a big black stove. The Reverend smiled at them from his seat at the scarred wooden table.

Moses looked around the room and got a lump in his throat. *This be what freedom look like. We be like family for the Reverend and his wife.*

"Sit down, boys. While the missus serves you some stew, tell me about your dog."

"We run off. Through a dark woods," Moses said.

"And we 'most got ate by a catamount." Tom shuddered as he remembered how scared they had been.

Moses leaned down to pat Cornpone. "But the Good Lord send us that dog and he chase the catamount away."

Granny Annie set a bowl of stew in front of each boy, one on the floor for Cornpone, and then served her husband and herself.

"Sit down, my dear," the Reverend said. "Let us pray."

Moses closed his eyes and prayed along. *Lord, you brought us safe this far. I know we be safe all the way rest.*

As soon as he heard the word amen, Tom attacked his stew as if he feared someone might snatch it away.

"I like to see a good appetite, but slow down, son." Granny Annie patted his hand. "There's plenty for a second helping."

Tom kept spooning his stew at a steady pace.

Moses pointed to the slices of bread. "That's the purtiest bread I ever did see. We just have cornbread all the time."

Granny Annie handed him a slice and the dish of butter. "Here's for your bread."

He stared at the unfamiliar yellow stuff and scratched his head. "What do I do with that?"

The Reverend hid a chuckle behind a cough. "That knife there beside your bowl, it's called a butter knife, so you can slice a dab of this butter." He demonstrated with his own knife and bread. "And spread it on. Makes the slice of bread into an edible work of art." He grinned and took a large bite.

After dinner, he pushed back his chair. "I can tell you've had a rough time. What about staying here to rest up for a few days?"

"I'd like that. All this runnin' make me tired, and I be tired to start out with," Tom said.

Moses shook his head. "Slave catchers be findin' us everywhere. We stay here and next they come knockin' on your door. Like the man in the plaid shirt today."

"I kept an eye on Mr. Bailey after you went to the cellar." Granny Annie stopped washing dishes and wiped her hands on her apron. "He walked past our house twice, staring. He never knocked, but I agree with Moses. It's not safe to stay too long."

"Tomorrow is the Lord's Day. Even ungodly men have a respect for God's house," the Reverend said.

"The Stone Church will be safe for the boys," Granny Annie said.

The preacher pushed back his chair. "Our church family will welcome you for the service."

Granny Annie's eyes sparkled. "Be like old times to have youngsters in our family pew. My own grandkids live far from here."

Tom ducked his head and looked sideways at her. "We have to dress up again?"

"I'm afraid so. None of our church members would turn you in, but we might have visitors," the Reverend said.

Moses remembered his joyful time in the brush arbor church. *I'd like to hear singin' and praises. Keep me from worryin' about slave catchers.* He smiled at the Reverend. "Even if we have to wear our girl dresses, Tom and me be ready tomorrow. Right, Tom?"

"All right. If there be singin'. I like singin', so's I can remember Grampa," Tom said.

Granny Annie had busied herself at the sideboard. "This will help you sleep well." She set a cup of milk and a square of gingerbread in front of each of the boys.

Tom's eyes got big and Moses blinked back tears.

"Where's mine?" the Reverend asked.

Granny Annie patted his arm and shook her head. "None for you. It's too rich for your diet."

Will's Trick

Ripley, Ohio

The Butler family marched to the Sunday service at Reverend Rankin's church and heard him preach again. This time, Pa nodded instead of frowning when the preacher spoke of the cruelties caused by slavery.

Will admired Reverend Rankin for preaching this unpopular message. He looked at those around him and wondered how many had changed their minds recently. *My own family has changed. But I don't see the slave catchers here. Or Cutter. And I don't see our nosy neighbor, Mrs. Williams.*

On the way home, the family walked together along Front Street. The river sparkled in the spring sunshine. Polly shepherded Hope and Charity, who had stopped to pick violets.

Will's mind followed a train of thought triggered by something he'd heard in the sermon. He stopped short as an idea popped into his head. *What if I gave false information to the slave catchers? They would hunt somewhere else for Tom and Moses instead of Red Oak.*

Will increased his stride to catch up with his parents. "Pa, where do the slave catchers stay when they're in Ripley?"

"Planning to make a social call on them?" His mother raised her eyebrows.

Polly joined them. "Will, why on earth would you want to talk to them?"

Will shook his head and smirked. "I'm following Pa's footsteps and hatching a plan."

"They share a room at Mrs. Gilliland's Boarding House." Pa put his arm across Will's shoulders. "What have you got up your sleeve?"

"Pa, when you left town yesterday, you thought Mrs. Williams might figure out it was Moses and Tom with you, not Ma and Polly." Will smiled as he thought of his idea.

"That's true."

"And if she told the slave catchers, they could figure out you'd headed north to the next town."

"Right. Those men still might head to Red Oak."

"What if we sent them an anonymous note saying the boys had gone somewhere else?"

Pa shook his head and rubbed his chin. "It would work better if the information came from Mrs. Williams."

Ma thought for a moment and beamed. "How about if I invite the neighbor ladies over for afternoon tea and give some hints about a different destination?"

"Or, I could say something and you could shush me, but not before Mrs. Williams heard," Polly said.

"However we do it, I want to send those slave catchers off on a wild goose chase," Will said.

Red Oak, Ohio

"Mammy be laughin' if she see me now." Tom grumbled and pulled at the neckline of the dress.

"Hurry up! Don't forget your bonnet. Smell that ham a-cookin'?" Moses said.

Tom put on his bonnet just as they heard Granny Annie calling them to come out for breakfast. The jars clinked when she moved them aside so they could wriggle through the low doorway.

"You boys should decide on girl's names, in case I have to speak to you in church."

Moses pointed to Tom. "I'll make up one for you, and you think of one for me."

Tom grinned and poked Moses' cheeks. "Dimples, 'cause you got them, right there and there."

Moses looked around the cellar and caught sight of a flowered curtain. "Rose. Tom, you be Rose."

"Dimples and Rose, good. Now you need to learn to curtsy."

"Hunh?" Tom shook his head.

"What be cur-see?" Moses asked.

"Curtsy. Young ladies bend their knees to show respect when they're introduced to a grown-up." Granny Annie held her skirt to one side and dipped toward the floor.

Moses lifted his skirt and tried a curtsy. Cornpone came to sniff under the edge of the skirt, so Moses put it back down. "You try, too, Tom. It ain't hard." They practiced a few more times, then headed up to breakfast.

The Reverend greeted them with a big smile. Granny Annie put one hand on Moses' shoulder and her other hand on Tom's. "This is Dimples, and this is Rose, for your information."

He winked at them. "Now I'm surrounded by the fairer sex." He waved a hand over the table spread with ham, eggs, biscuits, and hot tea. "Let's ask the Lord's blessing and you can practice eating in a ladylike manner."

Moses thought the mealtime prayer seemed especially long. He kept peeking at every pause, thinking it was finished.

Tom sneaked glances at the food and licked his lips.

After the amen, Granny Annie spread her napkin on her lap. Moses noticed and copied with a napkin on his lap. He elbowed Tom and pointed toward the napkin, so Tom spread his napkin on his lap, too.

Granny Annie watched Tom stuff his mouth full of ham. "Are you forgetting to eat like a young lady? Smaller bites, and slow down, please."

Tom hung his head. Moses stopped eating, with a bite in mid-air.

Granny Annie laughed. "It's hard to remember your manners when you're hungry. There's plenty of time for a second helping."

The Reverend finished his breakfast and pushed back his chair. He patted Cornpone's head. "We better leave the dog at home."

"Yessir," Moses answered.

"At church you'll be seated with the missus in the front pew. I'll give you the same warning the angel gave to Lot's wife."

Moses stopped buttering his third biscuit. "What?"

"When God destroyed Sodom, Lot's wife was warned not to look back."

Tom's eyes widened. "Did she obey?"

"She did not. She was turned into a pillar of salt. So, don't look back." The Reverend's stern look softened. "Facing forward will keep you from being recognized as runaways. Your description was on handbills all over Red Oak."

Moses put down his biscuit. *Not hungry anymore. Like to forget that. But best remember.*

"I doubt if anyone will try to grab you inside the church, but stay close to us after the service. We'll be the last to leave."

While the dew was still on the grass, the four of them filed to the stone church. The Reverend took the boys to the cemetery behind the church. "I want to show you the gravestone of the man who pastored this church before me."

Moses looked for an opening in the three-foot-high stone wall all around the little cemetery. "How we suppose to get in?"

The Reverend chuckled. "Don't try the way they got in—carried inside a casket." He stepped over the wall and turned to help the boys.

Tom started to run away, but tripped on his gown. "I be scared of buryin' places. They be full of dead people."

Moses grabbed him. "They not goin' to hurt you. Just lift your skirt and climb over."

The Reverend crossed to the center with long strides. He stopped before a plain gravestone. Moses and Tom stood beside him, wondering what the words said.

"In Memory of Reverend James Gilliland, Born 1769, Died 1845. Faithful Minister, Good Citizen, Ardent Abolitionist, Lover of Liberty, Friend of the Friendless."

Moses reached to touch the Reverend's arm, but drew back. "You be a-followin' his footsteps, sir."

"With the Lord's help, I try to fill his shoes." He turned and loped toward the church. "Let's get inside so we can get you a front row seat."

Granny Annie took the boys by the hand and led them to the front pew. Moses stroked the smooth wood. "These be mighty fine seats for the likes of us."

She sat down and patted a spot beside her. "Sit down. We're all equal in the Lord's sight."

The boys slid into the pew and Tom looked around. Moses poked him. "We ain't allowed to look back, 'member?"

Moses heard the hum of conversation behind him, but stared straight ahead. *Never been in a white church. They got a fancy chair for the preacher. And a stove for heat.*

He leaned over and whispered to Granny Annie, "What be that low bench up front?"

"That's a mourner's bench. A praying place for people sad over their sins. Hush now, we'll talk later."

Moses mused on the mourner's bench. *Didn't need no bench last Sunday. Lord, I be sad for my sin. But next I got the joy of Jesus.*

A bearded man in a black coat stood at the front and raised his arms. "Let us all stand and sing 'Amazing Grace.'"

Moses sang the hymn with a smile on his face. *Yes, I once was lost and now am found. Tom and me went through many dangers, but you promise to lead us home, Lord.*

The Reverend stood behind the pulpit and opened a very large Bible to read aloud. "God hath made of one blood all nations of men for to dwell on all the face of the earth."

As Moses listened to the preaching, his mouth dropped open. *God say we be just the same on the inside. Be that true? How come black people be slaves and get whipped?*

Moses was used to hearing "Amens" and "Hallelujahs" during preaching, but no one shouted out in this church. *Maybe people don't like the preachin'. I sure do like it.*

After the service, two older women came up to the front of the church. Moses and Tom wanted to run away, but Granny Annie held their hands. "Dimples and Rose, I'd like you to meet my friends, the Campbell sisters." She leaned over and whispered, "Don't worry, they won't turn you in. Now's the time to curtsy."

Tom and Moses stood, nodded, and curtsied.

The two ladies, both about Granny Annie's age, smiled. "Welcome to Red Oak Church," the shorter one said. Her sharp eyes took in every detail.

"You behaved like perfect young ladies," the other said, pulling her shawl tighter around her bony shoulders. She turned and winked at her sister.

Granny Annie reached into her beaded pocketbook. "Dimples and Rose, you deserve a reward." She handed them each a peppermint.

The three ladies chatted for a long time. They discussed what was simmering for Sunday dinner, where they'd gathered their first wild greens, and when a certain young lady in the church would receive a proposal of marriage.

Moses sucked on his peppermint. *These ladies figured we wasn't girls. But they didn't make no fuss we was colored.*

The Reverend waved goodbye to the last of the congregation and called to his wife. "Let's get home and eat. I'm half-starved!"

As he strode into the kitchen he told the boys, "I saw Jack Bailey in the back pew this morning. After dinner we need to figure out where you're headed next."

Goodbye to the Reverend

Red Oak, Ohio

Moses and Tom leaned forward to catch every word when the Reverend gave them warnings and directions. "It's a long way to Canada, perhaps two hundred and fifty miles. You may have to walk part of the way, traveling at night. You'll be hungry, thirsty, tired, scared, and ready to give up. But the missus and I will pray every night for you."

"Won't nobody help us?" Tom's voice trembled.

"Yes, many will help, even feed you and give you rides. Others will leave food under a wooden box with a rock on top. But be careful. Be suspicious of everyone."

"How can we tell if a house be friendly?" Moses asked.

The Reverend sketched a picture of a black boy holding a lantern in his hand. "Ever see a statue like this?"

"Nope."

"A figure like this out front of a house might hold a lantern or a flag. Either way, it's safe to knock on the door for help."

Moses pointed to the sketch. "But if it don't hold nothin'?"

"Keep right on going. Another signal it's safe to knock on the door, a candle in an upstairs window."

Granny Annie came in and spoke in a low voice to her husband. "Jack Bailey is walking back and forth out front again. Need to be extra careful when these boys leave."

The Reverend frowned. "You boys keep out of sight in the daytime. The slave catchers will be looking for you."

"Lots of things to worry about," Tom said.

"You can make it, with the Lord's help." The Reverend stood and stretched. "You have half a day to rest and get ready. We'll talk more tonight before you leave. Right now, I'm ready for a nap."

"Me, too, soon's I get me out of this dress," Tom said.

In the cellar, Moses asked Granny Annie about the books in their room.

"Go get the whole stack. Let's get started learning how to read."

When he returned, she opened a book with colorful drawings and a few words on each page. "Let's try this one."

While Tom napped, Moses and Granny Annie spent the afternoon reading. When they finished, Moses felt like dancing. "Mammy be so proud of me if she hear me readin'."

"Let me give you a big hug for your reward."

Tom, done with his nap, crawled out of their room. "You been lookin' at books this whole time?"

"I been *readin'* books," Moses said.

Granny Annie handed a book to Moses. "The best way to remember your lesson is to teach Tom all you learned."

Moses waved the book at his cousin. "You hear, Tom?"

"Take the books back to your room. It's about five hours till time to leave," Granny Annie said.

In the room, Tom began to shiver. "I got the prickles. I be gettin' sick."

Moses squinted at his cousin. "You sure you ain't just scared?" He paced around the room, as if he were already on his way. Cornpone tagged along at his heels, casting his silent vote with Moses.

"I ain't well enough to leave." Tom moaned about pain in his head and pain in his chest.

Moses put his hands on his hips and frowned. "Stop whinin'. We cain't stay here forever."

"I ain't ready."

"You never be ready!"

"Just one more day?"

"The slave catchers kin come in here any time and snatch us back to Kentucky. You want to see Cyrus again?"

Tom rolled his eyes and grimaced. "Only if I be the one with the whip and he be the one tied to the tree."

Moses voice got louder. "You be afeared of the dark?"

"Plenty to be afeared of."

"We got to be brave."

"Something evil goin' to happen." Tom clutched his chest. "I got a bad feelin' right here."

"We be delivered from dangers already. The Lord, He keep on deliverin'."

"You do talk about the Lord plenty," Tom said.

They heard footsteps. Moses lowered his voice. "If you talked *to* the Lord more, keep you from worryin'."

Three taps on their sliding door cut short their argument. "You ready, Tom and Moses?" Both boys flinched when they heard their names called by the Reverend.

Moses crawled out. "Yessir." Cornpone slipped out behind him, wagging his tail.

Tom crawled out, grumbling, but added his own "yessir" a moment later.

The preacher gave them a stern look. "Did I hear you boys arguing?"

Moses hung his head. "Tom and me, we don't always see eye to eye."

"You boys'll face many dangers out there. Many men want you back in chains." The Reverend made a chopping motion with his hand. "If they can divide you, they will win. Work together to outwit them."

"Yessir." Moses nodded and put his hand on Tom's shoulder. *He be right. Tom and me, we only strong together.*

The preacher handed them each a cloth bag. "Here's bread, dried meat, and a bit of money."

"Thanky. You folks been mighty kind," Moses said.

Tom clutched his bag. "Reverend, say goodbye to Granny Annie from us."

"She'd be here, but she's upstairs watching out the window for Jack Bailey." He led them through the basement and up stone steps to a wooden trapdoor. When he lifted the door, they saw a sliver of moon in a night sky studded with stars.

Moses sucked in a deep breath. "Look at them stars."

The Reverend pointed to the brightest star overhead. "Every night your guide is the handle of the drinking gourd."

Moses and Tom studied the sky and nodded.

"The next small settlement north of here is Sardinia. Turn left on the fourth side street to a brick house with a chicken painted on the door."

"Fourth street and a brick house with a chicken." Moses turned to his cousin. "You say it, too, Tom."

"Fourth house with a brick chicken. No, a brick house with four chickens." Tom shook his head. "Tell me again."

"Now I be mixed up, too." Moses scratched his head.

"Go to the fourth street in town, turn left, and look for a brick house with a chicken painted on the door," the Reverend said.

Moses and Tom both practiced repeating the directions.

"Go to the back door and knock three times. Say, 'a friend sent me.'"

"What if we cain't find it?" Moses asked.

"Sleep all day in the woods. Stay out of sight. The slave catchers won't give up."

Tom hung back, a worried look on his face.

"Any more questions?"

"What city we goin' to at the end?" Tom shivered and hugged himself.

"Sandusky. The last city in Ohio. It sits on Lake Erie."

"Next be Canada, the Promised Land," Moses said.

"Let's pray before you go."

All three sent prayers to heaven, and then Moses, Tom, and Cornpone plunged into the darkness.

22

The Made-Up Map

Ripley, Ohio

On Monday morning, Ma and Polly baked teacakes, cleaned house, and sent invitations to the neighborhood ladies. They covered the well-worn table with a linen cloth and unpacked the best teacups. Polly helped dress her little sisters in clean gowns, and tied ribbons in their hair. Poor Jonah felt left out, so Polly promised him a special party of his own if he played by himself in his bedroom during the party.

Before he and Pa left for work, Will pulled Polly aside. "Here's the map. I drew the Ohio River and made up an address near Cincinnati, marked safe house."

After a glance, Polly folded it and slid it into her pocket. "When I serve the guests their cakes, I can drop it near Mrs. Williams."

←——○——→

When Will and Pa arrived at the foundry, Will asked Mr. Parker if he knew whether the slave catchers were still in town. "Sure they are. They've been asking around for information about our two young fugitives. I don't think they've found out anything yet."

Will didn't give any details of the trick he'd planned, but asked his boss to let him know of any new developments.

Will chuckled as he worked, imagining the party, the planted map, and the slave catchers going on a wild goose chase.

At noon Will and Pa enjoyed eating lunch in the spring sunshine. Cutter sat nearby eating and laughing with his friends.

"Pa, will Mr. Cutter ever change his ideas about slavery?"

"Doesn't seem likely."

"Would he ever come to hear Reverend Rankin preach? That's one way people change."

"Oh, like me. I was halfway in agreement before we went to his church."

"Mr. Cutter acted brave when he and his friends raided the Rankin's house."

"The liquor made all of them bold," Pa said.

"What if we challenged him to see if he'd be brave enough to go to Reverend Rankin's church?"

Pa glanced at Cutter, then at Will. "Why don't you ask him?"

Will looked at Cutter and went back to eating. "Maybe I will. But not today. Guess one wild idea at a time is enough."

Over supper, Ma and Polly pronounced their tea a success. "We might make it a regular springtime event," Ma said.

"Mrs. Williams picked up the folded map, looked at it, then slipped it into her pocket without a word," Polly said.

"I'd sure like to know if the trick worked." Pa leaned back in his chair.

"Even more, I'd like to know how Moses and Tom are doing," Will said.

Night Journey

Red Oak to Sardinia, Ohio

Moses and Tom hiked for an hour, staying far enough off the road to be out of sight. The sliver of moon gave enough light to find their way. The few houses they passed were dark and quiet. Once a dog barked and ran toward them. Cornpone growled. Both boys sprinted, crashing through the underbrush till the barking stopped.

As they continued north, the road narrowed to a single lane. They hadn't seen a house in a long time, just fields and trees, so they walked on the road.

Tom kept close to his cousin. "Them trees full of shadows. Glad Cornpone be with us."

Moses began to hum his favorite tune.

"We be walkin', not ridin'," Tom grumbled.

Softly, Moses sang the words to another favorite. "'Go down, Moses, 'way down in Egypt Land. Tell old Pharaoh, Let my people go.' Tom, don't your heart just jump for joy? We be on the way to freedom."

"We ain't there yet. Lot of bad things gonna happen."

"You just a big worrier."

"The Reverend say we got two hunnerd and fifty mile to walk. My feet hurt already."

"We got a long way to go, for sure. But music make time go faster," Moses said.

The two hiked along, with Moses humming and Tom listening.

Tom stopped when they walked past a pond full of noisy spring peepers. He tilted his head. "Those peepers be a-sayin', 'stop here, stop here, stop here.'"

Moses laughed. "No, they be a-sayin', 'keep it up, keep it up, keep it up.'"

Tom perched on a fallen log and began to eat. "I'm not listenin' to no frogs." He tossed some bread to the dog.

"We never gonna get there, stoppin' all the time," Moses said.

"Mose, I be homesick for Mammy and Pappy. Ain't you homesick, too?"

"That place ain't my home no more. We run off. Now let's get goin'."

Tom dragged himself to his feet and the two plodded along in silence. Mile after mile they put one foot in front of the other. Moses convinced Tom they'd better not stop again. The sky grew a shade lighter, so they slipped into the woods, but continued northward.

The boys stopped short when they heard a horse and wagon coming down the road. Heart pounding, Moses pulled Tom behind tall bushes. Crouching low, they saw the dim outline of a man with a broad-brimmed hat. A single horse pulled a wagon loaded with hay.

After the wagon passed, Moses slipped toward the road. "We near the town. Let's go find the house with the chicken picture."

"Somebody gonna see us." Tom hung back, hiding behind the bushes.

Moses grabbed Tom's arm. "C'mon. Hurry afore it be all the way light."

They worked their way toward the cluster of buildings. The street ahead had shops on both sides, with few trees or bushes to hide behind.

Tom grabbed Cornpone's rope and hunkered down in the shadows. "You go hunt the place by yourself."

"No, we got to stick together." Moses pulled Tom forward. "We got to count four streets." They ran down the main street and turned down the fourth one.

Tom complained with every step. "We gonna get caught, for sure."

"Keep goin' till we see the chicken."

A dog began to bark ahead. Tom held Cornpone's rope even tighter.

"There. That be the right house." Moses pointed to a two-story brick house with a large chicken painted on the front door. They ran around to the back where a large dog leaped and barked at them.

"This house ain't safe." Tom dropped Cornpone's rope and ran back around the side of the house, Moses at his heels.

Wondering about Cornpone, Moses peeked around the side of the house. A spotted dog twice as big as Cornpone strained at a chain. Moses gave a little laugh when he saw the two dogs nose to nose, wagging their tails. "C'mon, Tom. That dog be tied."

Moses took a deep breath and edged to the door, Tom trailing behind him. The dog began barking again. He knocked three times and waited, staring at the knob. Several minutes passed and their knees began to wobble. Tom clutched Moses' arm as the doorknob slowly turned. Moses felt like he might faint.

A young girl, her long brown braids tied in blue ribbons, peeked out at them.

The boys stared open-mouthed for a long moment, then Moses stammered, "M-mornin', Miss. A friend sent us here."

She smiled and nodded. "Come in, friends. Ma's upstairs. Thou must leave thy dog outside, but I'll feed it when I feed ours." As soon as they stepped inside, she turned and ran, leaving the two boys to wonder if they should follow.

Moments later, she returned with a tall woman dressed in brown homespun, with a white cap and collar. "Thou go back to bed, Belle." She smiled at the boys. "Hello, friends. Did anyone follow thee?"

"No, Ma'am. We seed nobody," Tom said.

"We walk all night from Red Oak. The Reverend tell us about your house."

"Follow me." She led them down a long hall to a parlor. After closing the door, she slid a hidden panel aside to show a ladder nailed to the wall. "Thou will be safe up there. Eat the food, sleep in the beds, and we'll send thee on thy way after dark tonight."

As the boys climbed the ladder, she warned them, "Keep quiet. And be careful not to knock thy heads on the low beams."

"Thanky, Ma'am," Tom said.

The steeply slanted ceiling of the attic room kept them hunched over until they sat down on the bench in the middle. Both light and air leaked between the end boards under the gable roof. Several beds piled with blankets sat in the center of the room. In one corner was a washstand with a pitcher of water. Under it was a chamber pot.

"Pretty fancy," Tom whispered.

Moses grinned when he saw food set on a table. "Let's pray so's we can eat."

"You pray for both of us."

"Thanky, Lord, for this food and for the girl who be goin' to feed Cornpone, and for this family bein' kind to us. And nobody catched us. Amen."

As they munched on carrots and brown bread, Tom grabbed a round purple-topped vegetable. "Mmm. Turnip." Moses dug out the knife and sliced crisp rounds for each of them.

With full bellies, they stretched out in the beds under the gable. "Mose, you be right," Tom said.

"'Bout what?"

"The Lord be watchin' out for us. But we got a long way to go."

24

Wagon Full of Hay

Sardinia to Hillsborough, Ohio

Moses and Tom awoke to see the bright-eyed girl with braids staring at them from the top of the ladder. It took them a minute to remember where they were.

"Time to wake up," she said. "It's almost dark." She set down a large bowl of oatmeal and a smaller bowl of applesauce.

"Your name Belle?" Moses smiled at her.

She nodded. "I fed thy dog. What's its name?"

"Cornpone."

"That's a funny name." Belle's giggles tumbled out and filled the little room. "When thy food is eaten, come down the ladder, but stay in the back room."

The tall lady of the house met them and handed them some corn cakes. "Here's for thy sacks. My husband is getting the wagon ready to take thee to Hillsborough. May the Lord go with thee."

Moses thanked her and they headed to the barn. Belle held the team of horses while her father loaded the wagon with a layer of hay. The boys nodded a greeting to her.

Her father, a stern-looking man with a beard, handed them each a triangle of fabric. "Tie these rags around thy nose and mouth. I'm going to cover thee with hay."

Tom and Moses snickered at each other once they had their bandannas in place.

"Climb in, boys. Then keep thine eyes closed." They scrambled into the wagon and stretched out on the hay. He pitched loose hay over them till they couldn't even see the dim light of the lantern on the post beside the wagon. "I'll let thy dog walk behind the wagon. Keep thy heads down the whole trip. Slave catchers passed through today."

Moses shuddered at this news. He heard Belle say goodbye to her father.

"Belle, tell Mother I aim to be back before sunup." He clucked to the horses and the boys heard the soothing clop, clop, clop of hooves on packed ground.

Moses whispered to Tom, "This wagon be like our chariot."

"This ain't the Promised Land."

"But we still headin' north."

They could hear a few night sounds above the clatter of the horses. Bawling cows signaled they had passed a barnyard. Later, owls hooted as they passed through woods. Even though their bed of hay wasn't thick enough to shield them from the bumps of the rutted road, after a while they both fell asleep.

They were jolted awake by a man barking an order. "Drive the whole wagon into the barn." Unseen hands pulled off the hay. "Let's get you boys settled before we get any visitors," said a pink-cheeked man in suspenders. He led them to one of the stalls in the well-built barn. He raked straw away from a section of floor and pulled a ring to lift a trap door.

Moses and Tom stared into the black opening. Tom gulped. "We 'spose to go down there?"

The driver of the wagon, with Cornpone at his heels, held the lantern over the entrance so they could see stone steps. "I saw some men on the road just before I turned in here."

The pink-cheeked man motioned them down the stairs. "Hurry. It's a stone room with mats and blankets. Some food there, too." He lit a candle from the lantern and handed it to Moses. The boys and their dog climbed into the dark hole, with a wave of thanks to the two men as they replaced the floor overhead.

Moses held the candle high. "Look, a mat with a star quilt."

"That one be for me." Tom dove onto the bed and looked around. "We be safe from slave catchers here?" He grabbed Cornpone and held him close.

Moses reached for the tin breadbox. "Maybe. If we be quiet, and blow out the candle soon."

Tom munched on his cornbread and gave a low moan. "All the time we be runnin' away and hidin' in the dark. Something bad be comin', I feel it."

"Quit your frettin'. Whatever bad thing come, we in the Lord's hand." Moses stretched out on a bed and prayed himself to sleep.

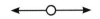

John Parker's Foundry, Ripley, Ohio

Wednesday, when Will and Pa went to work, Mr. Parker assigned them the task of loading a wagon out front. As they hefted the heavy parts into place, Mr. Parker joined them. "I have news of the slave catchers. Late Monday I saw them leaving town, heading west."

Will grinned. "Good. We drew a fake map so a neighbor would give them some false information and send them toward Cincinnati."

"But now they're back in town. They swore they'd find the two boys from Simon Anderson's farm. They're beating the bushes for clues on where to hunt them."

Pa shook his head. "Half of Ripley will give them information for a price. Every leg of their journey is dangerous."

Mr. Parker pushed his cap back. "True, but Ohio is crisscrossed with underground railroad lines. In ten days or so, those boys will probably land in a port town on Lake Erie."

Will grunted and grabbed another box. "Wish we could find out if they make it safely to Canada."

Mr. Parker nodded and rubbed his chin. "I've got contacts in Sandusky. Likely they'll end up there. I'll send word for my friends to keep an eye out for the boys."

"I'd appreciate that." Will smiled and gave him a grateful look. "I worry about them. They deserve to be free."

25

Next Leg of the Journey

Hillsborough to Washington, Ohio

Tom and Moses woke with a start when they heard the trap door open above them. Bits of dirt and straw showered them. A shaft of light from a lantern showed the same pink-cheeked man smiling down at them. "It's dark. Time to head north again."

Moses poked Tom, who groaned and turned over in his bed.

After a few minutes, they climbed the stairs with Cornpone at their heels. "We be ready," Moses said. The two horses in their stalls neighed softly at them, as if the boys were disturbing their sleep.

The farmer shook his head and gazed in the direction of the first horse. "I'm not ready, sorry to say. My big horse is lame. So I can't take you to your next station." He shifted his gaze to the boys. "Follow the road to Washington. Of course, stay off the road. There's a big woods along the way, too. In town, look for the big white mill building. A ruined stone house behind it looks abandoned, but has fresh water, food, and beds."

"How far?" Moses asked.

"It's a good twenty-five miles. Lots of farms along the way. Don't walk through plowed fields, either. Footprints."

The man handed them each a loaf of bread wrapped in a cloth. Tom licked his lips. "We thanks you, sir."

The farmer peeked out the partly opened door. "I saw a shadow when I came in here. Stay hidden in the stall until I make sure the coast is clear."

He returned after many minutes. "Looks good. Get goin'." He pointed them north and they slipped along the edge of the barn to the jumble of trees that edged the road. Cornpone, eager to explore, ran ahead, sniffing the ground. The moon made just enough light to see the road.

"Not many hills. Make walkin' easier," Tom said.

"Easier to plow, too."

"I don't like plowin'."

"Me neither. But I liked Ol' Pete."

"But I do like eatin'. When we be free, I find me a good wife to plant a garden and fix my dinner."

Moses shook his head. "You still have to work at somethin'. Me, I aim to learn blacksmithin'."

"I remember Ol' Jacob, did the smithin' for Master Simon. He sure have big muscles."

"I use to watch him makin' things. He bend the iron like magic."

Tom chewed a bite of bread and waved the rest at Moses. "Baker. That be a good job for me."

"Maybe not. Iffen you eat too much of what you be bakin'." They both chuckled.

Long and empty fields stretched ahead of them, and they plodded on and on. The fields gave way to trees, then to thick woods.

The shadows of the tall trees wavered in the moonlight. Tom shuddered. "You go first."

Keeping the road in sight, the boys threaded their way through saplings and underbrush.

Tom stopped and tilted his head. "Listen. I hear somethin'."

Moses, heart thumping, listened for a moment. "It ain't like a animal noise. More like somebody a-wailin'."

"Gives me the creepy-crawlies. I don't like it."

Moses pointed to the right. "It be comin' from deeper in the woods there." Cornpone disappeared into the trees to investigate where Moses pointed.

"I'm not goin' in there. Let's run instead of walkin'." Tom matched actions to his words and took off running like a catamount was after him. Moses sprinted behind him until they both stopped, panting for breath.

Tom looked all around. "You still hear it? "

"Yep. But it ain't slave catchers, so we ain't got nothin' to be scared of." Moses put on a brave face.

"Could be haints. I got to get out of this woods." Tom started running again.

Moses ran to catch up. "Ghosts go faster than people runnin'. It sound more like people, anyway." The boys raced along the edge of the woods, tripping on roots, getting scratched from branches and brambles.

Tom ran faster. "Haints can sound like anythin'."

Moses slid into a stream, lost his shoe, and cut his foot on a sharp rock. Tom tried to pull him out, but tumbled into the water. Sopping wet, they dragged themselves out the far side and sat on the bank, panting and listening.

"There be the noise again. Sound like a baby cryin'," Moses said.

"Look." Tom grabbed his cousin's arm. "'Way off in the woods there. Somethin' white!"

Moses gulped. "Let's stay still. I cain't run no more nohow. My foot be hurt." He drew up his right foot to show the gash on the bottom still dribbling blood.

"I got to get away." Tom clawed his way to the top of the stream bank. He ran, putting distance between himself and the noise, between himself and the white something.

"Don't leave me." Moses crawled toward Tom.

Tom stopped and leaned against a tree, ready to run.

Moses stood and limped toward him. "Wait. I can cut me some bark strips to bind my foot." He stripped a ribbon of bark from a sapling and wrapped his foot with it. He peered into the darkness, fearful of what he might see. He jumped straight up when he felt a cold, wet something push into his hand. Cornpone's nose.

The noise became louder and closer. Tom grabbed his cousin's arm. "There. The white shape. It be a haint for sure." He bolted away, swallowed by the dark woods.

Moses began to hobble after his cousin, but looked back when he heard crying. Five dark forms trudged through the woods on the other side of the stream. A flash of white from one of the shapes made his heart stop and his hands turn cold. He couldn't make his legs move, but stared as the figures moved along. Except for that cry, they were silent as death.

Moses called out to Tom, but his voice sounded like a sick kitten. He watched in horror as one figure turned toward the stream. *That shape, it look like Tom. It be his ghost, for sure.*

The figure knelt, took a drink, and stood up. Moses sucked in a big breath and let it out, the first breath he'd had in several minutes.

The figure heard the noise and looked toward it. The boy stared at Moses across the stream. "You goin' to Canada?"

Moses nodded, then looked around for his cousin. "Me and Tom."

"Us, too. We been runnin' for a week. Slave catchers almost got us, twice now."

A woman's voice called out, "Elijah. Who you talkin' to?" The woman, in a raggedy dress, carried a whimpering baby wrapped in a white blanket.

"Another runaway, Mammy." Elijah went on to explain to Moses how his baby sister was sick and they'd have to find medicine soon or she'd die.

Moses nodded and thought of his own sick baby sister. She'd never recovered, even though Aunt Bess had brewed roots for her medicine. "We be headin' for Washington, the next town on the road. A man told us about a mill and a safe house behind."

"Can we come, too?"

"You can come, but it ain't my place. I got to find my cousin Tom. He ran off, 'cause he think you was ghosts."

At this Elijah laughed and ran to tell his family. Moses limped off after Tom. Both sets of fugitives headed the same direction, in sight of each other. The moon, high in the sky, showed that night wasn't quite over. The woods thinned. Ahead, farm fields stretched to meet a huddle of buildings.

When Moses and Tom heard horses cantering down the road, they shrank back into the underbrush beside a field. Two men on black horses trotted past them. Elijah and his family were hidden in the brush on the opposite side of the road. The baby had been quiet an hour, but now her fretful cry began again.

"If them be slave catchers, that baby goin' to be the death of them all." Moses shook his head.

The horsemen continued on into town. Elijah raced across the street to ask Moses and Tom about medicine in Washington.

The boys shook their heads. "We hear nothin' about medicine," Moses said.

"I got to find a doctor," Elijah said.

Tom crossed his arms. "I ain't goin' into that town. Slave catchers there."

Elijah started toward the town. "If I go there for the doc and never come back, you know it ain't safe."

Both groups watched Elijah disappear into the line of trees near the town. Moses stretched out to rest his throbbing foot. Tom pulled out his half loaf of bread and stuffed bites into his mouth. Cornpone's sad eyes earned him a few bites of the precious food. The sky grew bright as the sun peeked over the low hill beside the town.

Tom frowned at the sky. "We cain't hide here all day."

"Let's go back to the woods."

"Yep. That be a safer place."

"Even with haints?" Moses grinned.

Tom started to answer, but was interrupted by the sound of galloping horses. "Slave catchers!"

Moses sucked in a breath. "They got Elijah and be comin' for us."

Across the road, the other fugitives dashed toward the woods.

Tom covered his eyes. "They gonna get caught!"

"Quick! Hide in the blackberry thicket." Moses pointed to a patch of brambles. The boys dove into their cover moments before the horses thundered past.

Tom's eyes bugged out. "Poor Elijah. I seed him tied behind that second slave catcher."

Moses stared down the road, watching an awful scene unfold. Elijah's family sprinted in all directions as the men chased them on horseback. The mother stumbled and fell, holding her baby close. One slave catcher dismounted and raced toward them.

"They caught his mammy and the baby!" The mother's sobs tore into Moses' heart.

"The pappy and two more chillen be comin' to help. They gettin' caught, too," Tom wailed.

Moses knees knocked and his stomach tightened. He watched the slave catchers tie the whole family in a line and haul them behind the horses. He closed his eyes. *Oh, Lord, please help Elijah get loose again. Please keep his baby sister from dyin'.*

"We be next, for sure," Tom groaned.

Where to Next?

Near Washington, Ohio

Moses and Tom spent the whole day in their hiding place in the blackberry patch. Moses unwrapped his foot and let the sun shine on it. Cornpone left to go hunt himself some dinner. The boys took turns taking naps in the shallow beds they scooped in the soft dirt under the arching brambles. When Cornpone returned at dusk, the boys made plans to leave.

"Poor Elijah and his family," Tom said.

"They might get loose again. I prayed for them."

Tom looked for the fifth time in his burlap bag. "My stomach be growlin'."

"Maybe we can get food from the safe house in the town."

The two waited till full dark and crept toward the town. Moses still limped. The gash in his foot looked awful and every step gave him pain. The two-story mill loomed over them as they glided around the back to a tumble-down stone house. They gobbled crackers and dried meat they found there. What little was left they stashed in their burlap pokes for their journey.

Beyond the town, the boys and their dog kept on heading north, following the road. They walked all night, watching for signs that a house might welcome fugitives.

Near morning, Tom spotted a candle in an upstairs window. "Maybe this house be safe?"

Moses nodded and pointed. "A church next door."

A dog began barking and the boys grabbed Cornpone, shrinking into the shadows to watch. A young man holding a candle came to the door and looked into the darkness. "What is it, Boots? Are you telling me there are friends out there?" The dog walked to his master to get a pat on his head.

"The man have a black coat. Maybe a preacher." Moses pulled Tom forward. "C'mon."

"You go first." Tom held back.

The boys edged toward the man, who looked up to smile at them. "Don't be afraid. Our home is the Lord's, so it's open to you."

Moses and Tom came closer, giving the strange dog a wide berth.

"Don't be afraid of Boots, boys. She's trained to let us know when someone's coming. I'm Brother Dickey."

"We got a dog, too. Can he stay?"

He held the door open for them. "Boots likes company, too. Come join us for breakfast."

Moses, Tom, and Cornpone followed him to a back room with benches and a table.

A red-haired boy and a younger blonde girl climbed up on the bench across from them and murmured a shy hello. Their father rumpled the boy's hair. "Run and tell Mother we have company for breakfast. Both of you help Mother with the food for these two hungry boys."

Brother Dickey looked at the boys. "Am I right?"

Moses and Tom smiled and Tom rubbed his stomach.

"Tell me your names."

"I be Tom."

"I be his cousin Moses. We been walkin' all night."

Brother Dickey glanced at Moses' bare foot. "What happened to your shoe?"

Moses lifted his sore foot to show the gash. "It come off when I slid into the creek."

"Son, that foot needs attention. I'll be right back." He soon returned with soap and water, salve and a bandage and set to work. "There. That gash will heal better now."

"Thanky, sir. It be painin' me the livelong night."

Mrs. Dickey and the two children returned with a jug of milk, a big plate of ham, and thick slices of bread. The red-haired boy put a dish of scraps on the floor for Cornpone. Brother Dickey thanked the Lord for the food and for bringing the runaways to his door.

Moses and Tom tried not to gobble their food. The Dickey children leaned forward to watch every bite.

Brother Dickey bent down to pat Cornpone. "You all are probably tired from your long walk. We'll bed you down for the day, then take you to the next station tomorrow morning."

"We be grateful for all your kindness, sir," Moses said.

"Thank the Lord. He's the one who directs me to offer a cup of cold water to the one who's thirsty."

Later, as they fell asleep in their hayloft beds, Tom heaved a big sigh. "It's a wonder them slave catchers didn't catch us yesterday."

Moses felt a lump rising in his throat as he thought of Elijah and his family. "We might get caught yet. But if we do, maybe the Lord have a reason."

←—○—→

Washington, Ohio

The early-morning sun slanted through the slits in the barn siding and woke Moses. He jostled Tom and Cornpone, curled up together. "Wake up! We slept too long."

Below, he heard Brother Dickey talking to his horses. "Eat your oats, Barney and Bill, we're taking a trip today."

Moses leaned and waved. "We be ready, sir."

"Good morning, boys. We're heading north in the carriage to visit friends in Columbus. The Keltons. You'll ride along in style."

Moses scrambled down the ladder.

Next Tom zipped down. "Don't leave without me."

Cornpone looked down from the loft, whimpered, then jumped into a pile of hay.

Brother Dickey set down a jug of milk and a platter piled with pancakes. "Have some breakfast. We'll start in a half hour or so."

Later, the Dickey family marched into the barn and Brother Dickey hitched up the horses. Mrs. Dickey greeted the boys and pointed to the carriage. "Climb on inside. Mary Elizabeth and I will ride inside, too."

Tom's jaw dropped when he realized that he and Moses would be riding in the fancy carriage he'd seen parked in the barn.

"This be our sweet chariot, for sure." Moses grinned and poked Tom.

Brother Dickey climbed into the driver's seat. "Samuel, you'll help me drive. Shall we let the dog ride with us, too?"

Samuel grinned and opened his arms to Cornpone. His father helped them both into the seat beside him. The dog curled up at the boy's feet.

As the carriage rolled out of the barn, Mrs. Dickey pulled the shades closed. "We need our privacy today." As soon as they left town, she raised the shades and pointed to the spring wheat showing green in the fields they passed.

Mary Elizabeth snuggled up to her mother. "Tell us a story, Mama."

"That's a good idea. We'll be riding all day, so we'll have time." She began with the story of her great-grandfather traveling to Ohio on a flatboat.

As he listened to the family stories, Moses got a lump in his throat. *All my family stories be sad ones. When we get to Canada and freedom, things be different.*

Mrs. Dickey turned to the boys. "Tell us how you escaped."

Mary Elizabeth's eyes opened wide as Tom began the story. "In the woods, we hear a catamount a-screamin'."

"We be mighty scared. But the Lord, he send us a brave dog," Moses said.

"And he chase that catamount away." Tom clapped his hands.

Moses told about Mr. Parker rowing them across the Ohio River at night. As Mrs. Dickey encouraged them, the boys opened their hearts, pouring out the details of their lives.

Moses told how his mother learned to read from another slave scratching letters in the dirt. Tears came to his eyes as he described the whipping she endured for teaching her son to read.

Both Mrs. Dickey and Mary Elizabeth had tears in their eyes, too. Mrs. Dickey put her hand on Moses' shoulder. "When you get to Canada, maybe you can go to school."

Around noon, the carriage stopped near a grove of trees. They enjoyed a picnic lunch, and then walked to a nearby stream to stretch their legs before the next leg of the journey.

Mrs. Dickey closed the shades again as they got closer to Columbus. "Our friends Sophia and Fernando Kelton built a house on the edge of the city. They wanted to be able to help slaves escape to Canada."

The Keltons had a fine house and two barns. They welcomed Tom and Moses, fed them, and settled them in the upstairs servants' quarters.

Moses sank down on the feather tick. "Tom, seem like everywhere we go, kind people help us."

"That be true." Tom nodded and frowned. "But slave catchers be everywhere, too."

Moses peeked out a tiny window when he heard squeals of joy. He could see the buildings of a city off in the distance. The Dickey children raced around a grassy lawn, playing hide and seek with the younger Keltons. "Back home, we never get to laugh and play like that."

Tom came to look out. "Cyrus get to play. He play crack the whip to make sure we keep workin'."

"When we be free, we have fun, just like that." Moses had a faraway look in his eyes.

"*If* we be free. We ain't there yet."

Halfway to Canada

Columbus, Ohio

Brother Dickey brought them their breakfast the next day. He sat down to chat with them as they ate. "Your next stop will be Westerville with Bishop Hanby and his family. They'll treat you well."

Tom wiped his mouth after a big drink of milk. "How many more days till we be in Canada?"

"That's hard to say exactly, but I'd guess nine or ten days. Today you'll ride with Mr. Kelton in the false bottom of his delivery wagon."

Tom frowned and rubbed his head. "A bumpy ride."

"But safe. Let's pray before you head north." Three heads bowed as Brother Dickey asked the Lord to protect them.

Mr. Kelton burst into the barn. He stuffed a hat on his head, covering his wind-blown hair. Behind him, the breeze stirred a cloud of dust. "That dark sky threatens rain. Let's get moving and maybe we can miss the worst of it." He pointed to the opening in the back of the wagon. "Soon as you climb in, we'll close the door. I've got my goods packed already."

He hitched up two dapple-gray horses and climbed into the driver's seat. Brother Dickey helped the boys into their hiding place and slid the door closed behind them. "No room for your dog. He'll walk behind."

The boys crawled in and settled on the blankets. Moaning, Tom grabbed Moses' hand. "This be just like a coffin!"

Moses tried to calm his cousin by reminding him they'd traveled like this before. Tom clutched him even tighter. "I cain't catch my breath. I be goin' to die!"

"Grab some air." Moses pulled Tom to the breathing hole he'd found.

Tom filled his lungs with air. Moses began to sing. "Swing low, sweet chariot, comin' for to carry me home."

Tom relaxed his grip and sighed. Soon he began singing along.

They could hear the raindrops hitting the wagon. The smell of wet earth reminded Moses of home. "Remember the time we went fishin' and it start rainin' cats and dogs?"

"Thunder and lightnin' skeered me so bad I crawled in a holler log. And stayed till the sun came out."

The boys told each other stories and then sang. When they'd sung every song they knew, Moses patted Tom's arm. "We be headin' to the Promised Land. We have trials on our way, for sure."

"How come you ain't worried?"

"Way back before we run off, the Lord grabbed ahold of my heart. The preacher show me how I be a slave to sin. I hate Cyrus for whippin' me and whippin' Mammy to death. Preacher say, 'Repent. Grab ahold on Jesus.' So I did. Now I be God's child. He be sure to take care of me."

"I hate Cyrus, too. Since I be gone, Cyrus probably whippin' some other poor soul." Tom's voice had a hard edge, as if that memory cut through all other memories. "I hate him across the miles we run."

"Then you be draggin' a hate-chain behind you, even while you be runnin' to freedom."

"Don't you hate him, too?"

Moses realized that the angry hatred he had felt for Cyrus was gone. He shook his head. "Not anymore."

Tom squeezed Moses' hand. "I be needin' prayer."

"Yep, I pray. But you pray, too. And grab ahold of Jesus."

"I want to be God's child, too." Tom squeezed his cousin's hand again.

Spatters of mud reached their breathing hole. The rhythmic sound of the horses clopping through the puddles made Moses start to sing again. "Swing low, sweet chariot."

Tom's voice, trembling at first, joined him. "Comin' for to carry me home."

Westerville, Ohio

A young man's cheerful face greeted Moses and Tom as they crawled from their cramped quarters in Mr. Kelton's wagon. "Come out and stretch your legs, friends."

As soon as Moses and Tom climbed down, Cornpone ran to jump on them, wagging not just his tail, but his whole body. Tom lifted him up and hugged him.

Moses noticed an enormous workbench stretching nearly the length of one side of the barn. He wondered about the rows of tools and leather straps. Stalls lined the other side. A large black and brown dog stood guard at the doorway.

Mr. Kelton unhitched the horses to lead them to food and water. He shook water off his hat. "You two had a drier ride than I did! Good thing the sun finally came out." He turned to the young man. "Ben, this is Tom and that one's Moses." He pointed with his head as he gave the horses their grain. "Boys, this is Mr. Benjamin Hanby."

The young man's friendliness made Moses feel welcome. "Are you boys hungry, too?" he asked.

Moses nodded. "Tom be always hungry."

"Dinner will be ready in a half hour. Before then, I'll cover the windows in our house with black paper to make it safe. Meanwhile, you can wash up in the basin in the corner there. And there are clean clothes on the back shelf, too." He looked at Tom's worn-out shoes and Moses' bare foot. "And find yourself some shoes there, too."

"Thanky, Mr. Hanby," Moses said.

"Ben. You can call my father Mr. Hanby. Actually he's Bishop Hanby, but I'm just Ben." He leaned down to pat the dog. "What's your dog's name?"

"Cornpone." Tom bent down to scratch behind the dog's ears.

Ben laughed and turned to go, patting his own dog on the way out. "This is Towser. He'll guard the barn tonight after I lock up." He turned to Mr. Kelton. "Fernando, we've got plenty of food. Won't you stay for dinner?"

Mr. Kelton pulled a little book from his jacket pocket. "I hope to have dinner with an old friend who lives in town. I'll come in and say hello to your family, though."

After the two men left, Tom and Moses washed and changed, wondering aloud at the fact they'd be eating with the family. Tom shook his head. "Good thing we got some new clothes. Else I be 'shamed to set down at table with 'spectable folks."

"Yep. My old shirt ain't good for nothin' but a scrub rag."

After dark, Ben took them to the house and introduced them to his family. Moses and Tom nodded to each of the seven Hanby brothers and sisters.

Bishop Hanby, Ben's father, had a gray beard and a twinkle in his eye. He shook hands with them. "When I was your age, I was next thing to a slave. They called me an indentured servant, but treated me like a slave. I ran off to Ohio, just like you boys did."

Mrs. Hanby came up behind them. "Come sit down. I'm sure you're hungry. The food's not fancy, but there's plenty of it."

"Thanky, Ma'am," Moses said.

Tom ducked his head toward the loaded table. "Look like everythin' I like, Ma'am."

"That's 'cause he like everythin'," Moses said.

After dinner, Moses and Tom joined the family in the parlor for family devotions. Moses eyes got large as he watched Ben press his hands on parts of a large wooden box. *Music be comin' out of that box, but how?*

Tom leaned over to whisper to Moses, "What be that box?"

Moses shook his head. "Sound like angel harps, maybe."

"That hymn is one of my favorites." Mrs. Hanby patted Ben's shoulder.

The boys joined in the singing when Ben played a hymn they knew.

Bishop Hanby opened a large Bible. "Let us read in Deuteronomy. 'Thou shalt not deliver unto his master the servant which is escaped from his master unto thee. He shall dwell with thee, even among you, in that place which he shall choose in one of thy gates, where it liketh him best: thou shalt not oppress him.'"

Moses could hardly believe his ears. *This really be in the Bible? How come all them white folks in Kentucky never heard it before?*

Bishop Hanby's next words echoed Moses' thoughts. "Oh, that men in our nation would hear and obey God's Word."

After they sang more hymns and Bishop Hanby prayed, Ben led them back to the barn. When Towser bounded out to greet them, Tom hid behind Moses. "That hound friendly?"

"He knows his job is to protect all my friends. You're my friend, so he's friendly," Ben said. "But if you're trying to hurt my friends, he's a fierce one to face."

Moses reached a hand out to pat the dog, so Tom did, too. "Yep, he a friendly one. Our dog Cornpone friendly, too, but fierce with a catamount." The boys told the story of their brush with a wildcat.

Ben handed them each a blanket. "Tomorrow morning, just before sunrise, you will walk one block east and one block south to the Alexander Rake Factory." He held up some pieces of folded paper. "I'll set out a trail to follow. These papers will be at the corner of each street, to point the way."

"Mr. Alexander, he expectin' us?" Tom looked worried.

"Yes, he'll have a place for you in his tool delivery wagon," Ben said.

"Just like our ride yesterday? I feared I be dead and ridin' to the graveyard in my coffin," Tom said.

"Now, Tom, we cain't complain. We safe and dry and headin' north. That's the way I sees it," Moses said.

"I see it that way, too. Goodnight, and I'll see you in the morning." Ben locked the barn door as he went out.

Moses snuggled under his blanket next to Tom and Cornpone. Just as they were dropping off to sleep, Towser barked six short barks. Cornpone growled.

Tom grabbed Moses' arm and they both strained to listen. They heard footsteps running away. "Somebody tryin' to catch us."

"Towser keepin' us safe," Moses whispered. "The Lord, too. He keepin' us safe, all night long."

"Tomorrow sure to bring trouble. I feels it," Tom said.

The Rake Wagon

Westerville to Mount Vernon, Ohio

Ben brought breakfast to Tom and Moses before sunrise and gave them each a batch of corncakes for their bags. He fed Cornpone and Towser while the boys ate.

Moses leaned toward Ben. "Those hymns sure be pretty yesterday. That music sound like angels playin' harps in heaven."

"What you call that box what make the music?" Tom asked.

Ben's laugh made Towser's tail wag. "That's called a piano. We're blessed to own one. It's like a little bit of heaven to sing God's praises with my family."

Moses squeezed his eyes shut to keep the tears back as he remembered singing hymns in the brush arbor with his mother and the others.

"Back home, we have two banjos. But I do like that piana." Tom stood and stretched. "Now, tell us again about the papers pointin' the way?"

"Each turn has one of these." Ben showed them a sample of the folded paper. "One block east and one block south. Head toward the sunrise."

Moses tilted his head toward Tom. "We thanks you, Mr. Ben."

"God be with you both till we meet again. Even if that's in heaven."

As they made their way through quiet streets, Moses admired the neat yards lined with spring flowers. In the few blocks to the rake factory, Cornpone investigated many smells.

When the boys and their dog arrived, Mr. Alexander had his wagon half packed with rakes and hoes. "'Tis a fine morning, is it not? Is this bonnie puppy yours?"

Tom nodded and patted Cornpone's head.

"He can ride beside me and keep me company."

Mr. Alexander helped the boys into their hidden compartment with a warning. "'Twill be a bumpy ride, lads. The ruts are deep after last week's rain." He closed the cover. Moses and Tom heard thuds from tools piled on top to hide the compartment.

"I got the coffin feelin' again." Tom grabbed Moses' arm.

After the wagon jerked to a start, Mr. Alexander started singing. Tom's grip loosened. "Mr. Alexander, his singin be loud, but it be good."

Even in their compartment they could hear the words. "My Bonnie lies over the ocean, My Bonnie lies over the sea. My Bonnie lies over the ocean. Oh, bring back my Bonnie to me. Bring back, bring back, oh bring back my Bonnie to me."

"That song, it keep goin' on and on." Moses began to hum along.

"I be tired of it already," Tom said. "Ain't you?"

"We can make up our own words." Moses thought a while and sang, "My grampa live over the river, My grampa he work but ain't free, My grampa live back in Kentucky, I wonder when Grampa get free."

"I like them words, Mose. Let me try." The wagon bounced over a rut and Tom's head connected with the wood. "Oww. I cain't think." After a few fumbling tries, he finally began singing. "My mammy live over the river, I want to go back there to see, My mammy she live in Kentucky, …"

Tom stopped and left the last line for his cousin.

"But Canada's only for me."

Both boys were quiet as the driver continued his serenade.

Finally, Moses tried again. "My cousin he hear someone cryin', He say, 'they's a haint by the tree,' The cryin' be only a baby, But Tom run away from me. Come back, come back, oh, come back my cousin, to me, to me. Come back, come back, oh, come back my cousin to me." Moses hooted at his cleverness.

"No fair. Make a funny one about you, Mose."

"Hmm. Let me think."

"About the time we dress up like girls."

Moses mumbled a while, then sang, "Moses he dress up so pretty, with bonnet and gown and lace, He sure cain't walk like a lady, instead he fall on his face."

"I be glad we be done with our dressin' up," Tom said.

The horses clip-clopped and Mr. Alexander sang about his Bonnie.

"Mose, sometime I thinks we never goin' to get to Canada," Tom said.

"Oh yes, we will," Moses said.

"How can you be so sure we gonna get there?"

"I knows it in here." Moses put a hand over his heart. "Sing this one along with me. Our new home be north of Ohio, In Canada we both be free. I maybe go back to Kentucky, And bring others north with me."

Many hours and verses later, the wagon came to a stop. Mr. Alexander helped them out. "End of the line, boys." Cornpone frolicked around their legs, glad to see them again. "Get inside quickly."

Tom and Moses stepped inside a storage shed filled with empty crates. Mr. Alexander unlocked a cabinet and stashed the rakes and hoes in it. "There's a jug of water in the corner. Lay low here till I get back."

As soon as he was gone, Tom stretched his arms up over his head. "I been layin' low too long already."

Moses peeked outside through a wide space in the boards. "Mr. Alexander sound a mite worried to me. We best find a hidey hole."

They collected the jug of water and wedged themselves behind a stack of crates and waited. Tom rubbed his stomach. "Got anythin' to eat left in your bag?"

Cornpone stuck his nose in the bag when Moses felt for food. Moses found a few corncakes, which they shared.

It seemed ages before they heard Mr. Alexander. As if to warn them he was coming, the man sang his favorite song, My Bonnie Lies Over the Ocean. Inside, he called, "Hey, anybody here?"

Moses leaned out. "We right here, sir."

He strode back to their hiding place. "As soon as it gets dark tonight, go out to the main road and walk north about a mile till you come to a fence made of stumps. A man on a big white horse will pick you up. He lives north of here. He'll feed you and let you sleep in his barn."

Tom stared with his mouth open. "We be waitin' till then to eat, too?"

"I'm afraid so. I'll share my jerky with you before I head back to Westerville."

Tom grinned from ear to ear. Moses thanked Mr. Alexander for the ride and for the food.

They both stared through a crack in the shed at Mr. Alexander's wagon as it bounced away. After it had turned the corner they could still hear him singing his favorite song.

29

Horses Heading North

North of Mount Vernon, Ohio

Moses and Tom fixed themselves a bed in their hidden corner. They practiced singing their made-up verses to amuse themselves before curling up with Cornpone for a nap.

Hours later, Moses woke with a start. He sat up so fast he knocked his head on a board. "Ow. Tom, wake up. It be dark and we suppose to meet somebody on the road."

The two hurried down the road to the stump fence. They jumped when a shadow moved in the moonlight.

Cornpone sprang from Tom's side to chase a possum. "That possum be headed toward a creek to find dinner. Wish we had somethin' to eat."

"Ain't no man on a white horse here," Moses said.

"What we goin' to do?"

"We goin' to set right here till the man come along."

They perched on a log, listening to the crickets, the tree frogs, and the wind rustling the dry weeds. Tom complained how hungry he was, so they hunted some clover flowers, dandelion greens and onion grass to chew on. Cornpone pounced on several crickets for his dinner.

Tom waved his hand in front of his face. "We stink like onions. Nobody want us close."

"Nobody be comin' close anyway." Moses paced back and forth. "We better wait longer." They sat for twice as long as Tom wanted, but no one came.

"I be tired of waitin'." Tom checked the stars and headed down the road.

Moses and Cornpone joined him. Fields and woods stretched ahead, with an occasional farmhouse and barn.

Dawn had begun to color the sky when they heard horses coming. They jumped into the shadows of the undergrowth on the side of the road.

Moses peeked through the weeds. "Two men on horses."

"Comin' from the town we just left."

"One horse be white," Moses said.

Tom stood and took a step toward the road.

Moses grabbed his arm. "Two horses ain't the same as one. Stay back."

"Mr. Alexander say the man on the white horse be the one to feed us. I be hungry."

"Mr. Alexander say the man live north. These two comin' from the south."

"You stay iffen you want." Tom yanked his arm away and ran to the edge of the road. He waited until the bay horse passed, then stepped in front of the man on the white horse.

Both horsemen pulled their mounts to a stop. The man on the white horse leaned forward and pointed. "Ho, there. What's your name and what do you want?"

"Tom. I want some food and a place to stay."

Moses, still wishing they'd stayed in the shadows, stepped forward. The other man, on a bay horse, pushed his hat back and scratched his head. "Hey, there's another one. What's your name, boy?"

"Moses."

The man turned to his friend with a grin. "What say we help these boys out, Ike?"

Ike nodded, stroking his long moustache. "They'd fit on our horses just fine." He leaned down and offered his hand to Tom, who climbed behind him on the big white horse.

The other man nudged his horse toward Moses and reached his hand out.

Moses hesitated. "Where you goin'?"

The man tugged at his vest and leaned back, laughing. "You're smart to ask, boy. We're on our way to Sandusky to take care of business."

"Sandusky." Moses mumbled the name of the town under his breath. *I heared about it, but where? Somebody...the Reverend! That's where we get a boat to Canada.*

"We be goin' to Sandusky, too." Moses took a step forward.

The man offered his hand to Moses again and Moses climbed behind him on the big bay horse. Cornpone trotted behind the horses.

Moses by now had figured that these men had nothing to do with the man on the white horse who was to meet them the night before. He wondered if they had made a right decision to ride with them.

The four rode in silence, enjoying the stillness of the morning. At the next town, Ike stopped to post a letter.

Moses pushed away thoughts of what might happen once they reached Sandusky. He tried to appreciate seeing the trees and fields, the blue sky and fluffy clouds. *Don't usually see things in the daytime.*

After several hours, they dismounted at a stream to let the horses drink.

Ike, who seemed to be the leader, lifted the flap on his saddlebag. Tom drew closer. "Got any food in there, sir?"

Ike drew out a flask and took a big swig. He laughed at Tom and offered Harry a drink. "You boys should wet your whistle in the stream. We'll stop for lunch at some farmhouse. When we do, you boys pretend you're our slaves. Right, Harry?"

Harry nodded and took another swig. "Meanwhile, let's get moving. I figure it'll take a full two days to ride to Sandusky."

Moses whispered to Tom as they bent to drink at the stream. "I'm afeared we might really be their slaves."

"But they be headin' to Sandusky. And stoppin' to eat."

The four climbed back on the horses and headed north along the dusty road. When the sun rose high in the sky, Ike sniffed the air as they passed a farmhouse. "Mmm, smell that meat cooking? If my nose is any judge, we'll be well fed if we stop here." They tied the horses to the rail and Ike dug into his pocket for two silver dollars. He flipped them in the air as he walked to the door of the farmhouse.

Moses gawked. *Two silver dollars. A powerful lot of money.*

In a few minutes, Ike came back grinning, carrying a stack of bowls and spoons and a ladle. Behind him a plump woman carried a large pot of stew. Grunting, she waddled toward a bench.

Harry hurried up to her. "Ma'am, that pot is much too heavy for you. Let me carry it."

She gladly gave up her load, but her smile changed to a questioning frown when she saw Tom and Moses.

Seeing her look, Ike stepped forward. "We're headed to Sandusky on business, and our slaves have come along to help us. We're all mighty hungry."

"We greatly appreciate your kind hospitality," Harry said.

She smiled. "We just butchered a pig and I got more pork than I can process."

Ike waved his hand at the neat barn and outbuildings. "You have a fine spread here, Ma'am."

She beamed and adjusted her kerchief. "The Lord has blessed us, that He has. Now, you four can finish as much of that stew as you want and I'll get back to my kitchen work."

Harry thanked her again and began filling a bowl for himself. Ike did the same and handed the ladle to Moses.

Tom grabbed the utensil out of his cousin's hand. "Me first, before I starve."

Moses frowned, but let go of the ladle. After Tom finished, he filled his own bowl and one for Cornpone, too.

Tom shoveled meat and vegetables into his mouth, as if the pot might disappear before he got a second helping.

Moses shook his head as he studied Ike and Harry. *I wonder about these men. Why they bein' so nice?*

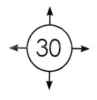

Slave Catchers Head North

Ripley, Ohio

The spring weather, with blossoming trees and fresh breezes, made Will smile as he and his father strode down Front Street on their way to work. The Ohio River sparkled and several fishermen cast lines from skiffs along the shore. That reminded Will of the last time he'd been in a boat, helping Tom and Moses to escape. "Pa, will we ever find out if those boys made it to Canada?"

His father looked across the water and shook his head. "I doubt it. We'll just have to trust they did."

Mr. Parker greeted them as they arrived at the foundry. "Meet me out front in ten minutes."

Out front, the foundry owner came right to the point. "Mrs. Gilliland, who rents a room in her boardinghouse to the two slave catchers, told me they left town yesterday. They're headed to Sandusky."

Will felt like a huge fist squeezed his chest. He cast a worried look at Pa. Tom and Moses would probably arrive in that same city any day now.

Pa shook his head. "Did Knight and Hughes ever find any information about those boys?"

Parker scratched his head. "I don't think so. But I don't really know. They might go to Sandusky just to see if they can snag a few runaways for the bounty money."

Will looked around, as if slave catchers might be lurking nearby "Is there anything you can do? Didn't you know someone there in Sandusky?"

"Yes, a business contact. I've already written to him to keep his eyes open for those boys. He runs one of the Underground Railroad stations in Sandusky."

"Could you ask him to watch for Knight and Hughes, too?" Pa asked.

"I'll post a letter today. Now let's get back to work before someone gets suspicious," Parker said.

Near Sandusky, Ohio

Moses and Tom continued riding on horseback toward Sandusky with Ike and Harry. Cornpone sometimes disappeared for a spell. Moses guessed he was chasing a rabbit. The road led through fields beginning to show new shoots of grain. At dusk they approached a village.

Harry twisted around to ask Ike, "We stopping at the Pine Tree?"

"Yep." Ike pointed to Moses and Tom. "Don't forget, you two play the part of slave boys."

Moses frowned, but nodded agreement. Tom licked his lips.

The Pine Tree Inn, a two-story white building, thronged with men and horses. None of the other travelers paid any attention to Ike and Harry and their slave boys. Moses had to admit to himself he enjoyed having regular meals. *Hope we get to sleep in a bed.*

The two men ordered spirits to wash down their stew, which made them talkative. Each imagined what they would buy with a large sum of money they expected soon.

The more Moses listened, the more suspicious he became. *They gettin' money from catchin' us. We got to escape. I tell Tom tonight when Ike and Harry be asleep.*

In the room, the men took off their coats and shoes and flopped on the lone bed. Ike laughed as he poked his buddy. "Harry, if your snoring keeps me awake, you'll find yourself on the floor."

Harry pulled a blanket over his shoulders and pointed at Moses and Tom. "The floor's already full. Just close your ears."

In a few minutes, both men snored so loudly it reminded Moses of Ol' Pete's braying.

"Wish I had Cornpone to snuggle with." Tom rolled up his burlap bag for a pillow and curled up along the wall.

Moses stretched out close to Tom. "Them men ain't our friends."

"What you sayin'?"

"I think they be slave catchers. Before we get to Sandusky, we got to run off."

"I ain't a-goin' back to walkin', nohow." Tom turned his face to the wall.

Moses gritted his teeth. *Lord, what's gonna happen to us iffen we stay with them?*

As they rode north the next day, Moses planned how they'd escape from Ike and Harry.

In the late afternoon, Ike pointed to a wooden sign. "Ten miles to Sandusky. I could've guessed we were getting close." He swatted at a cloud of mosquitoes around his head.

Harry looked down at the thick mud covering the horses' hooves. "Yep. This whole area's a bog. Glad I don't live here."

"The last ten miles may take three hours," Ike said.

"Maybe we should stop for dinner before then. My stomach's been rumbling."

Ike laughed and shook his head. "Do you see any farmhouses? If we stop, we'll be traveling in the dark. I never want to stray into this swamp at night. I've heard tales of men and horses lost and never found again."

"Guess I can gnaw on the beef jerky from my saddlebag," Harry said.

"Another reason we can't stop. Remember? We're meeting two friends."

Harry winked at Ike. "Yep. Don't want to miss that important meeting, do we?"

Moses, mounted behind Harry, missed the wink, but he guessed the meaning behind the words. *We be headed north now, but these men be goin' to send us south with slave catchers. Tom and me got to run now. That swamp be the place they won't never follow.*

Moses stared at his cousin. *Look at me, Tom.*

Tom finally glanced at his cousin. Moses pointed to himself and then to Tom and mouthed the word *run*.

Tom shook his head and looked away.

Moses clamped his jaw together. *If he don't come, I'm gonna run by myself. Take Cornpone with me for help.*

The mud on the road got thicker as they continued through the swamp. A sickening stench, like rotten vegetables, filled the air. Ike pulled his horse to a stop and waved to the others. "Call of nature. It's another hour till we get to town."

Tom and Moses went off together behind a nearby bush. As soon as they were out of earshot, Moses grabbed Tom's arm. "I'm runnin'. You comin'?"

Tom pulled away. "Why? You be crazy. I be afraid of this swamp."

Moses wanted to scream a warning, but he hissed instead. "They goin' to give us back to the slave catchers, to Knight and Hughes. I knows it. I choose the swamp."

Tom craned his neck at the two men, trying to decide. "Mose, they ain't slave catchers. They been kind to us. Don't leave me."

"I said, I'm runnin'. You comin'?" Moses grabbed Tom's arm again and squeezed tighter.

Tom pulled away. "No. You always be tellin' me, go here, don't go there."

"You be sorry. I get Cornpone, too." Moses spotted Ike heading back toward the horses.

Tom hesitated. "We almost to Sandusky. There be snakes in that place."

"Those men be the snakes. Cain't you see that?" Moses turned toward the swamp. "C'mon, Cornpone."

Tom set his jaw and turned toward Ike and Harry. "You got 'em all wrong."

Moses and Cornpone disappeared into the thick undergrowth. With every step, Moses feet sank down into the mud. Vines reached out to grab and trip him and the water came nearly to his knees. *This place gonna swallow me up. Nobody never see me again. But at least I be free.*

"Mo-ses. Git back here." Harry's voice floated over the swamp.

"He's running off! Get him!" Ike's shout had the hard edge of anger.

Moses plunged ahead, fighting his way through saplings and bushes. *They chasin' me. Sound like bulls crashin' through the trees. I thought they never come in here after me. They got Tom. They ain't a-gonna catch me.*

Ike raised his voice a notch louder. "Mo-ses. Come back. You'll never see the light of day again."

Moses batted at the clouds of mosquitoes swarming around his head. *Yep, I be already lost in this place. 'Spose Cornpone mebbe help me find my way back to the road? Cornpone? Where you be?*

He heard branches breaking nearby. *Ike and Harry ain't quittin'. Got to keep movin'. But I be makin' noise, too.*

Moses plunged deeper into the swamp. Panting, he sank to his knees and stopped to listen for the telltale noise of breaking branches behind him. All was quiet. His heart thumped and he gasped for breath. Shrill birdcalls sounded like a warning evil was close by.

A stone's throw away, Ike's voice shouted a threat. "Mo-ses! Come out now or I'll skin you alive."

Moses jumped up and tried to run again. *I be makin' too much noise.* Glancing back, he tripped over a root and fell with a splash into the gooey mud. He felt something wriggling under his hand. His heart skipped a beat. *Snake!* Panic welled up in his chest. *Lord, help me!*

Vigilance Committee

Reverend Rankin's Church, Ripley, Ohio

The congregation spilled out of the church and collected in groups on the lawn. The children danced around the newly-planted sycamore tree, playing follow-the-leader. Mothers stopped chatting long enough to warn their youngsters not to soil their church clothes.

Will and his father joined a group of men who spoke in voices tinged with anger. Reverend Rankin's sermon had recounted how a gang of men had barged into Thomas Collins' house one recent night to search for escaped slaves. Will felt angry for Mr. Collins, who had been kind to Moses and Tom.

Thomas Collins shook his finger in the air. "These men had no search warrant, yet they searched garret loft, privy, corncrib, henhouse, and barn. Even under our beds, though we had already retired."

"That's lawlessness," a tall man said.

Another man frowned and swept his arm around to include everyone in the circle. "We have to do something about it. It has gone on too long."

Thomas Collins leaned forward. "Big cities form vigilance committees, ready to defend the rights of citizens."

Father quietly explained to Will that a vigilance committee takes the law into its own hands when necessary.

"Ripley needs one as much as the big cities." Many nodded and added their own opinion.

"My name will head the list," another man said.

"Reverend Rankin, will you be our chairman?"

The pastor nodded. "Who will join with me?"

Will wanted to raise his hand. *Am I too young?* He waited to see what his father would do.

His father lifted his hand. "I'm in."

Others in the circle nodded or waved their hands.

Will glanced at his father, took a big breath and raised his hand. "Me, too."

Great Black Swamp, Near Sandusky, Ohio

Sprawled on his face in the mucky water, Moses looked up to see a big black snake lifting its head to strike. He snatched his hand back but too late. Moses cried out as the snake's fangs sank into the back of his hand. Moments later the snake slithered away. Moses clutched his injured hand and studied the bite. *Am I gonna die?*

He peered into the thick undergrowth. *Cornpone, where you be?* In the fading light, he thought he saw something moving. *Another snake? It ain't Cornpone.*

Moses stood to his feet and took a few steps away from the movement. The murky water made a sucking noise as he pulled his foot out. The other foot sank down, down, and Moses could not pull it out. He sank to his knees, heart thumping, as he struggled to escape. Terror welled inside him and he struggled harder to escape. The slimy mud had swallowed both legs. *Lord, don't let me die!*

Moses tried to grasp a scrubby bush, but it was just out of reach. The mud reached his waist and he kept sinking deeper. *Lord, I need your help!*

He stretched full length and concentrated on pulling one leg out. Each inch of progress cost five minutes of effort, but his right leg at last came free. Moses lay still to gather strength and then pulled his other leg out. He crawled on his belly away from the man-eating mud. He lay beside a tree, limp from the struggle.

The mud added so much weight that Moses couldn't even stand. He pulled off his shoes, shirt, and pants, rinsing them in a nearby puddle. With effort, he put them back on. *I need to get out of here. Which way? And where be Cornpone?*

As if in answer, he heard Cornpone barking. *Cornpone sound like he be ready to fight. What animal be scarin' him?*

His heart jumped into his throat as Harry's voice called to Ike from close by. "The kid and the dog went farther into the swamp. I hate going after them, but for two hundred dollars … ."

Moses tensed. *They think I be with Cornpone. Got to rescue Tom back at the road.*

Moses plunged away from Harry's voice, trying not to make noise.

Ike shouted, "Mo-ses. Come out. Or the alligators will eat you."

Moses snickered. *I ain't skeered of alligators. Just wildcats.*

Cornpone barked again, this time with urgency. *Maybe Cornpone be barkin' at a wildcat.*

Harry's voice sounded farther away, and angrier. "The mosquitoes are eating me alive!"

Moses looked at his throbbing hand. *It be swellin' up. Hope I be goin' toward the road.*

Ike shouted again to try to entice Moses to give himself up. "Mo-ses. Mo-ses. Tom needs you. He's begging and crying for you."

Moses held his throbbing hand and continued away from Ike and Harry's voices. *They just makin' that up out of whole cloth. They ain't anywheres near Tom. Or are they?*

When he broke through the underbrush to the road, the two horses quit munching the greenery and whinnied.

Moses groaned. *Tom ain't there. I got to run without him.*

The shouts from Ike and Harry no longer sounded far off. Moses ran toward the horses. *Stealin' a horse be bad enough to get me shot.*

Cursing, Ike burst out of the swamp. Harry emerged next, dragging Tom behind him on a rope. Cornpone bounded out last, barking at the men who had seized his friend Tom.

Moses made a quick decision. He raced to climb on Ike's horse. "Giddyap!" He smacked the other horse to make it run away. *Tom say he like Harry and Ike. Stay with them.*

Gripping the reins, he dug his heels into the horse's side. *Bible say, no stealin'. This be just borrowin'.*

Ike lunged for the reins of the riderless horse, but fell on his face in the mud.

As the horses disappeared down the road, Harry shouted, "We'll get you yet!"

Heart pounding, Moses galloped toward Sandusky. *Tom be done for. Shoulda helped him get away. And Cornpone, too.*

The swamp stank. As soon as he got out of the gloomy place, Moses yanked back on the horse's reins. He slid off, patting his mount.

Though Ike and Harry were not in sight, Moses thought he heard a horse coming. He sprinted down the road toward some distant farm buildings. He climbed a fence and raced across a field toward a weathered shed. As he neared it, a farmer came out carrying a shovel. He took a look at Moses' frightened face and muddy clothes and guessed the situation. "Ach! I hide you quick."

He pushed Moses into the shed. There he lifted the lid of a grain bin and motioned him inside. The man's face crinkled into a smile. "Safe you vill be. Do not vorry." He shut the lid and locked it before leaving the shed.

Moses shivered. His hand throbbed. The mud on his clothes smelled awful and had rubbed his skin raw under his arms and between his legs. An ache of loneliness pierced his heart. He brushed away a tear. *Lord, help Tom get away. And forgive me for not helpin' him.*

Sandusky on the Lake

Sandusky, Ohio

Moses heard the farmer talking to Ike and Harry outside the shed. The farmer opened the door and said, "Keep heading down the road. Sandusky is not far now."

Ike stepped inside the shed. "Let me look around here. I saw him running across your field." The lock rattled on the grain bin. Moses quivered and his heart thumped so loud he was sure Ike could hear it.

"Your runaway couldn't get inside that bin. I keep it locked," the farmer said.

Harry shouted from outside. "Ike, hurry up. We'll probably catch the other boy on the way to Sandusky. I'm hungry."

Moses heard the two horses gallop away. *I be safe. But they got Tom.*

After a long while, the lid lifted and the farmer's face smiled down at him. "Climb on out." He began to pull Moses up, but stopped short when the boy cried out. "What happened to your hand?"

Moses held up his swollen hand for him to see. "Got bit by a snake in the swamp."

He leaned close to look. "I shall get Frau Slemmer, that is, my wife, to salve and bandage it." He scratched his head. "Those men were hunting a runaway. But they had one tied to their horse already."

Moses' face crumpled. "That be my cousin Tom."

"So you escaped but Tom did not?"

Moses nodded, not wanting to tell the details. "How will Tom git loose? Cain't you help him?"

"We have a vigilance committee." The farmer rubbed his chin. "They might be able to help. My name's Andreas Slemmer, by the way."

Moses poured out his story to his rescuer. When Mr. Slemmer heard of John Parker's part in their escape, he slapped his knee. "Why, John Parker's a friend of Hiram T. Bell, in Sandusky. I'll give you dinner and take you to Bell's station after dark. Meanwhile, sit tight in this shed."

A little while later, Mrs. Slemmer bustled in the door with a basket of food.

"*Guten tag*, good evening, Moses." She pulled out sausages, a jar of applesauce, and dark brown bread from her basket.

Moses' eyes sparkled when he saw the food. "Thanky much, Ma'am. I be mighty hungry."

"First let me fix that snakebite on your hand." She cleaned the wound, and then applied a white salve.

"Am I goin' to die from it?"

"I think not," Frau Slemmer said as she wound a strip of cloth around his hand. "Now you can eat."

Mrs. Slemmer smiled to see Moses' good appetite. "That sausage recipe came from my Grandma, back in Germany."

She pointed to a stack of feed sacks folded on a shelf. "After dinner, stretch yourself out for a nap. Andreas will be back in about an hour, when it's all the way dark." She disappeared out the door.

Moses smiled to himself. *Next time I have supper, maybe in Canada. Poor Tom. Ike and Harry goin' to haul him back to Kentucky.*

Later, Mr. Slemmer and Moses rode to town on the farmer's plow-horse. It didn't take long, since the muddy stretches of road had been lined with logs.

"Nellie gets skittish on this corduroy road." He patted his horse. "But it's a sight better than having her sink down to her withers."

Moses wondered what withers were, but didn't ask. Mr. Slemmer chatted on about finding the safe house, getting ready for the steamship ride, and how it was that Mr. Hiram T. Bell knew John Parker.

The city of Sandusky looked like an oversized Ripley to Moses. Houses and storefronts spread out along a big body of water, with more boats than he had ever seen at once.

Moses stared open-mouthed at the lake. "Mr. Slemmer, maybe we see Canada from here? I mean, if it warn't dark."

"Nein." The farmer shook his head. "But you'll see Canada soon enough. Up ahead is Mr. Bell's warehouse. He'll get you a steamship ride right across Lake Erie, probably tomorrow."

They tied the horse behind the warehouse. The night watchman challenged them until he recognized Mr. Slemmer. "Got some cargo for the ship, sir?"

Mr. Slemmer took Moses to a windowless room piled with crates of all sizes. He pointed to blankets and water. "Lock the door after I leave. You'll be safe here till Mr. Bell comes tomorrow. I'll ride by his house, up the street, to let him know he's got a passenger waiting."

Sitting in the dark, Moses strained to hear the street noises outside. A mouse scurried in one corner of the room. That reminded him of his cabin on Master Simon's farm. *I miss Grampa. He say he be prayin' for us. Aunt Bess pray special for Tom, so maybe he get loose. If he don't, it be all my fault.*

Moses' sleep swirled with guilty dreams of Tom calling for help. He was awakened by barking outside. *Cornpone!*

The door opened and a slender man with a curly black beard burst into the room. Cornpone danced at his heels. "Good morning, Moses. Is this your dog? I found him sitting out back."

"Yessir."

Cornpone, wagging his tail, pranced toward his owner. Moses hugged the dog and grinned. "You be Mr. Bell?"

"Hiram T. Bell, at your service." He handed Moses bread and beef jerky. "Bet you're ready for breakfast before your boat trip."

"I thanks you, sir." Moses sighed. "They suppose to be two of us goin' to Canada. Me and my cousin Tom. Two men say they bring us to Sandusky. But they was slave catchers."

"What were their names?" Mr. Bell crossed his arms and frowned.

"Ike and Harry."

"I've heard of them. Slave catchers camp out in Sandusky. In the past, they've even boarded ships with arrest papers." He pointed to a large crate in the corner. "That's why I pack you into a crate to load you onto the ship."

Moses peered sideways at the large wooden box.

Mr. Bell opened the top. "You and your dog will be safer in there than stretched out in a comfy chair on deck. In a few hours, the ship will leave the pier and head to Canada. Then the captain, he's a good man and a friend of mine, will open your crate."

Moses sighed and climbed in. "Wish Tom was comin' too."

Mr. Bell plopped Cornpone beside Moses before he nailed the lid closed. He called two workmen to carry the crate to a wagon.

Moses felt every jolt on the log-lined streets. The shrill cry of seagulls split the air as the crate was lowered from the wagon. Cornpone slid sideways into Moses when the crate thudded to the ground. *That fishy smell. Faraway splashes. This be the dock. Wonder when I get loaded on the ship to Canada?*

He rubbed Cornpone's ear, the one that wouldn't stand up. "I don't like it, Cornpone. Slave catchers come along and find us any minute." The dog licked Moses' cheek as if in sympathy.

Time dragged and Moses strained to listen. His stomach did flip-flops every time he heard a suspicious noise. The four walls of the box pressed against him. *Lord, are you watchin' over me? And what about Tom?*

The Good Shepherd

Henry Butler home, Ripley, Ohio

The Butler family gathered in their parlor for morning prayer. Ma knitted a sock and Jonah fidgeted at her feet. Polly, Hope, and Charity focused on Father as he read from his Bible. Will stared into space, imagining what bad things might be happening to Moses and Tom in Sandusky.

"In John, chapter ten and verse eleven, Jesus says, I am the good shepherd. The good shepherd giveth his life for the sheep."

Polly noticed her brother was not paying attention and elbowed him.

Father gave Will a stern look. "Can you tell us what Jesus meant by this verse?"

"Um, Jesus wants us to, er, love one another?"

Polly raised her hand, trying to hide a smile. "Can I say what I think, Father?"

"Please do. I'm glad *some*one was listening."

"When Jesus calls Himself the good shepherd, He means that we are his sheep and He will take care of us, even dying for us."

Father nodded, smiling at Polly. "Jonah, what is the shepherd's job?"

Jonah jumped up and swung his right arm in circles, pretending he held a sling. "Shepherds pertect their sheeps. They kill any wolves what come to eat them up." Jonah spoke the last three words with a menacing look, as if he were one of those hungry wolves.

Will raised his hand. "Can we pray that Jesus will protect Moses and Tom? I can't get them off my mind. They could be in danger."

Hope waved her hand in the air. "I get to pray for Moses." She pointed to her sister. "You can pray for Tom."

"I want to pray for both of them," Charity said.

Mother frowned.

Father cleared his throat. "We will all pray for both of them. Will's right. They need prayer, and lots of it."

Father began and each in turn prayed for Tom and Moses to get safely to Canada.

Sandusky, Ohio

Moses heard men's voices and his heart lurched. *Sound like Ike. And Harry.* He hugged Cornpone.

Nails screeched as unseen hands pried the lid from the crate. Ike's face glared down at him. Moses' heart stopped and he shrank into the corner. *I be done for now. Tom and me both goin' back to Kentucky.*

Ike's strong arm yanked him to his feet. "Aha! We caught him!"

Harry grabbed Moses' other arm. "The dog's here, too. Help me with this rope."

Cornpone bared his teeth and began to growl.

Ike drew a gun. "Call off your dog unless you want him dead."

Moses gripped Cornpone and lifted him out of the crate. "Go find Tom." The dog scampered away.

"You and your runaway pal will be together mighty soon," Ike said.

Rough hands dragged Moses out of the crate and tied his hands behind his back.

A man rushed from the ship, waving his arms and shouting. "Stop! What are you doing?"

Ike crossed his arms, as if daring anyone to stop him. "The law says we can apprehend runaway slaves. This one escaped from Kentucky and we're taking him back."

The man shook his head. "You can't seize him without papers."

"We're taking him straight to the courthouse." Ike yanked Moses toward the bustling street.

Harry, his thin face bright red, grabbed Moses' other arm and squeezed so hard Moses thought his arm would break. "You thought you'd get away, did you?"

Moses dragged his feet. In his mind he was back in Kentucky and Cyrus whipped his bare back.

Ike and Harry marched Moses five blocks along the waterfront to an old brick building. Moses caught sight of Cornpone skulking nearby. *Tom must be in there. Leastways we be together again.*

When the two men hauled Moses through the door, a bearded man in uniform looked up from his ledger. "Gentlemen, state your court business." He looked over his glasses at Moses as if it were nothing new to see someone with his hands tied.

Ike took a step forward and tapped the ledger. "This is the other runaway what nearly escaped to Canada."

"Yes, I recall now. You brought me a fugitive an hour ago. You must all appear before His Honor, the Mayor."

"When do we got to bring the two agents for their owner?" Ike asked.

The bearded man glanced at the nearby clock. "Mayor Follette begins the afternoon session in three hours, at one o'clock." He pointed down the hall. "Until the hearing, take this fugitive to room number five. The constable in charge will take good care of him."

As Ike shoved him down the hall, Moses' heart sank. *I be so close to Canada. I never goin' to get there now. Lord, please help.*

At the door of room number five, the burly constable opened his logbook. Ike filled in the blanks and handed the book back. The constable glanced at the writing and waved the two men away.

Ike grabbed Moses' ear and yanked it hard. "Don't try any tricks or you'll be sorry. We'll see you in a few hours with some old friends of yours, Mr. Knight and Mr. Hughes." He shoved Moses into the room.

At this news, Moses heart stopped. *Knight and Hughes. They be comin' to take us back to Master Simon's.* He stumbled into the room.

A second constable caught him and took him to a bench lined with other runaways.

Moses' jaw dropped. He could not believe the sight before him. *Tom. And Elijah. And Elijah's mammy, his pappy and his two brothers. His mammy be holdin' his baby sister. She ain't dead. Thanky, Lord.*

When he sat down, Moses leaned toward his cousin. He wanted to hug him, but his hands were still tied. "Tom. I be sorry. I run off without you."

"No, you be right about Ike and Harry."

"You be right about the snakes. I got bit." Moses wiggled his bandaged hand.

Moses leaned around Tom to nod at Elijah. "We meet again."

A commotion at the door made them all turn to see. Moses' eyes grew round when he recognized Mr. Bell. Behind him a group of both black and white men with stern faces crowded into the room.

One of Mr. Bell's gang who had arms like a wrestler motioned to the constable at the door. "Could I speak to you privately in the hall?" The stocky constable nodded and disappeared.

Mr. Bell came over and spoke to Moses in a low voice. "Which one is Tom? Both of you be ready to come with me in a minute." He glanced at the other constable, who watched them with sharp eyes.

Moses glanced at Elijah and his family, then back at Mr. Bell, asking a wordless question.

Mr. Bell scanned the crowd, counted, and started to shake his head.

Elijah's mother held out her baby. Her eyes pleaded her yearning to flee with them.

Mr. Bell nodded, then signaled to the rest of his gang. They pressed around the second constable and began asking questions.

"Follow me," Mr. Bell whispered. He slit the ropes tying their wrists.

Elijah grabbed a little brother's hand, his mother hugged the baby, and his father carried the other boy. They tiptoed out the door behind Moses and Tom. In the hall, the other constable faced away from them as he argued with the wrestler-man. The group had nearly reached the back exit when one of the constables shouted. "Stop! In the name of the law."

Mr. Bell grabbed the hands of both boys. "Run as fast as you can. The rest of my men will block the doors and delay the constables."

They all slipped through the door and raced toward the docks, Mr. Bell leading the way. Moses and Tom let out a yelp of joy when they saw Cornpone running beside them.

They dashed through back alleys, worried any minute someone would grab them and take them back to the courthouse. Panting, they reached the dock and saw the steamship Mary Anna preparing to pull up her gangplank.

Mr. Bell pushed through the crowd on the dock. "Wait!" The sailors stopped untying the thick ropes and stared at the band of fugitives. Nine men, women, and children and one yellow dog with a floppy ear filed up the gangplank. As soon as Tom, the last one in line, climbed aboard, the men pulled up the gangplank and cast off from the shore.

At the dock, four men pushed to the front of the crowd and shouted. They waved their arms for the steamship to stop, but it continued to glide across the lake.

Mr. Bell grinned at the nine escapees. "We made it! Follow me below." They climbed down a steep ladder to a narrow room with benches along both sides. "Not fancy, but safe. We won't be in Canadian waters for four or five hours."

Cornpone made friends with Elijah's two little brothers. They both hugged the dog, pulling it in opposite directions. Cornpone rolled on the floor, wriggling between them.

Elijah's mother rocked the baby, singing a soft lullaby.

"Listen to the steam-engine music." Moses leaned back, grinning. "It be singin' Can-a-da, Here I come, Can-a-da, Here I come, Can-a-da, Here I come."

Tom shook his head. "I believe it when I set my foot down on solid land. We been close before. Maybe somebody come aboard and take us back."

"Tom, you be such a worrier."

Elijah leaned forward. "If I'd worried more, maybe our family wouldn't got caught. But it be the best thing for my baby sister. The slave catchers gave her medicine and her fever went down."

Elijah's father patted the baby, still wrapped in the dirty white blanket. His deep voice throbbed in time with the ship's engine. "Let me tell you, boys. The Lord, He work it so the devil's wickedness get changed into good somehow."

Tom looked up from stroking Cornpone's ear. "That be true. We rode slave-catcher horses most way to Sandusky, 'stead of walkin'. And they fed us good, too."

Moses smiled at Elijah. "How did you all get to Sandusky? I thought I'd never see you again after you got caught."

"That be a long story. But we got plenty time." Elijah laughed.

The three boys enjoyed swapping stories while the ship chugged north. They laughed and cried and shared dreams for their new life.

Mr. Bell returned with cheese, bread and water. "Your first meal in Canada."

Moses had such a big lump in his throat he could barely speak. "Canada." Tears began to roll as he wrapped Tom in a big hug. "We made it to freedom. The Lord answered Grampa's prayer."

Sandusky, Ohio

Dear John Parker,

Rec'd your letter of the 14th instant, warning to watch for the bounty hunters, Knight and Hughes. They have been to Sandusky before, so I knew them by sight.

A farmer friend brought Moses to me. I packed him in a specially-made crate to be loaded on the Mary Anna. Before he could be transferred to the steamship, two slave catchers pried open the crate and hustled Moses to Mayor's court. Tom was there already, since he had chosen to stay with two other men who turned out to be slave catchers. Knight and Hughes planned to meet them there, to transport both boys back to Kentucky. I called on our vigilance committee, ready for just such emergencies. We rescued the boys, their dog, and even another family of fugitives from the courthouse.

I made the trip on the steamship with them, so I saw with my own eyes that they arrived safely in Canada.

Yours sincerely,

Hiram T. Bell

Letter from Canada

Ripley, Ohio

Summer 1855

Polly raced into the house, waving a letter. "Look, Will. This letter's to you. The handwriting has lots of curly-Q's. The return address, Buxton, Ontario, Canada. Who do you know there? Open it. Hurry up."

Will's heart leaped as he studied the envelope. "Fancy handwriting, but I bet it's really from Moses and Tom."

Polly put her hands on her hips. "If you'd open it you'd know for sure." She ran to get Pa's sword-handled letter-opener from his desk.

Will sliced open the envelope and held the page so Polly could read it with him.

Dear friend of Moses and Tom,

Moses wanted me to write to you so you'd know they are safe and happy in Canada. They live with me in Buxton, a community of former fugitives. Everyone here helps each other.

The Lord sent Moses and Tom to help this poor widow and now they are my sons. They will start to school in two months, but Moses wanted to learn how to read right away. He worked hard to write the letter to you, enclosed. He'd like you to write back. The address is on the envelope.

Yours truly,

Emma Jane Tucker

Polly grabbed the envelope and looked inside, finding a second sheet of paper.

She held it up for her brother and they read it together.

~~Dor~~ Dear Will,

We be in Cannada our dog too.

Tom and me got freedom what word

~~yu~~ you tot me insidte tree.

We hav a new mammy she say I need me 2 boys To help dig garden to help chop wood. She larn me riting.

Thanc ~~yu~~ you for hepping me and Tom.

Th Lord send you for shur

Yer frend,

Moses

Will grinned and gave his sister a hug. "They made it!'

Polly wiped a tear away. "I wish we could hear all about the adventures they had on the way."

"Maybe we will. Let's write back."

Polly ran to get pen and paper.

"Moses has his heart's desire. He knows how to read and write." Will smiled. "I think the Lord has big plans for him."

Author's Note

Some of the characters in this story really lived in 1855 and could have met our fictional heroes, Moses, Tom, and Will.

John Parker knew the evil of slavery firsthand. He earned his freedom and started a foundry in Ripley. He invented and manufactured plowshares and shipped them by steamship down the Ohio River. He crossed into Kentucky to conduct runaways to freedom, a dangerous task.

Reverend John Rankin's home on Liberty Hill above Ripley welcomed freedom seekers. He preached the message of abolitionism from his pulpit in Ripley and many other places around the state of Ohio. In spite of threats, he and his family continued helping fugitives find freedom.

Thomas McCague owned a pork-packing plant in Ripley. As he shipped pork south on the river, he helped fugitives north on the Underground Railroad.

Thomas Collins, cabinetmaker, made coffins as well. More than once, fugitives hid in his coffins. John Parker and two fugitives narrowly escaped from slave catchers that way.

Reverend James Gilliland founded a church in Red Oak, Ohio. He and his successors kept the welcome mat out for fugitives on their way north.

A Quaker family gave Tom and Moses food and shelter. Quakers were active in the Underground Railroad because they believed the Bible taught the equality of all men before God.

Fernando and Sophia Kelton built a fine house on the outskirts of Columbus, Ohio. They welcomed fugitives there, away from prying eyes of the city. Fernando's delivery wagon had a false floor for carrying slaves north to freedom.

The Hanby family of Westerville, Ohio befriended many escaped slaves. Benjamin was deeply touched by the story of one fugitive whose sweetheart was "sold down river" to work in the fields, never to be seen again. The ballad he wrote about this event later became very popular as a Civil War song.

Darling Nelly Gray
by Benjamin Hanby

There's a low green valley on the old Kentucky shore
Where I've whiled many happy hours away,
A-sitting and a-singing by the little cottage door,
Where lived my darling Nelly Gray.
Chorus
Oh, my poor Nelly Gray, they have taken you away,
And I'll never see my darling anymore.
I'm sitting by the river and I'm weeping all the day,
For you've gone from the old Kentucky shore.
When the moon had climbed the mountain, and the stars were
    shining too,
Then I'd take my darling Nelly Gray,
And we'd float down the river in my little red canoe,
While my banjo sweetly I would play.
Chorus
One night I went to see her, but "She's gone!" the neighbors say.

The white man bound her with his chain;
They have taken her to Georgia for to wear her life away,
As she toils in the cotton and the cane.
Chorus
My canoe is under water, and my banjo is unstrung.
I am tired of living anymore.
My eyes shall look downward, and my song shall be unsung,
While I stay on the old Kentucky shore.
Chorus
My eyes are getting blinded and I cannot see my way;
Hark! There's somebody knocking at the door.
Oh, I hear the angels calling, and I see my Nelly Gray,
Farewell to the old Kentucky shore.
Final chorus
Oh, my darling Nelly Gray, up in heaven there, they say,
That they'll never take you from me any more;
I'm a-coming, coming, coming, as the angels clear the way.
Farewell to the old Kentucky shore.

←—O—→

Mr. Alexander, of Westerville, had a business making garden tools. His delivery wagon had a secret compartment for carrying freedom-seekers.

The Great Black Swamp, in the northwest corner of Ohio, includes the area below Sandusky. Many snakes lived there. A non-poisonous three-foot-long black racer bit Moses. This corner of Ohio with its swampy ground could not be farmed until it was drained. In the 1850's, hard-working German immigrants used the abundant clay to make drainage tiles and successfully farmed the land.

Many slaves departed for Canada through Sandusky, Ohio, a shipping port on Lake Erie. Some ship owners, risking forfeit of their ships, gave free passage to runaways. By 1855, about 250,000 blacks had found freedom in Canada.

Buxton is a rural town in southern Ontario, Canada, established in 1849 by former slaves. They established churches and schools, farmed their own land, and even built a factory.

Vigilance committees, made up of private citizens, administered law and order when they considered government was not doing the job. They acted to help many fugitives on their way north.

The Underground Railroad had many lines in Ohio, with conductors and safe houses known only to those nearby. Both blacks and whites played active roles.

CPSIA information can be obtained
at www.ICGtesting.com
Printed in the USA
FFHW012342170219
50571316-55908FF